HARLEQUIN® *Presents*

2802
February

Nicola Marsh

THE BOSS'S
BEDROOM AGENDA

D0048293

HARLEQUIN *Presents*

Glamorous international settings…
unforgettable men…passionate romances—
Harlequin® Presents® promises you the world!

AVAILABLE THIS MONTH:

ISBN-13: 978-0-373-12802-0
ISBN-10: 0-373-12802-9

9 780373 128020

50475

EAN

HPATMIFC0209

HARLEQUIN®
Presents

Welcome to the February 2009 collection of Harlequin Presents!

This month read the final installment of Lynne Graham's trilogy VIRGIN BRIDES, ARROGANT HUSBANDS, *The Spanish Billionaire's Pregnant Wife.* Leandro Marquez ruthlessly stops at nothing to wed Molly when he discovers she's pregnant with his child! And don't miss the first part of our fabulous new series INTERNATIONAL BILLIONAIRES, which starts when shy, hardworking Holly is swept off her feet by the magnificent Prince Casper in Sarah Morgan's *The Prince's Waitress Wife.* Expect emotions to reach fever pitch in Carole Mortimer's *The Mediterranean Millionaire's Reluctant Mistress* when tycoon Alejandro is determined to claim his secret baby and possess Brynne in the process. And will an innocent plain Jane convince Sheikh Tair Al Sharif to let go of his mistrustful nature in Kim Lawrence's *Desert Prince, Defiant Virgin?* Business tycoon Santos Cordero is intent on seducing Alexa into a marriage of convenience in Kate Walker's *Cordero's Forced Bride,* while sexual tension heightens when Stefano seeks revenge after being left at the altar in Kate Hewitt's *The Italian's Bought Bride.* Be prepared for a battle of the sexes in Robyn Grady's *Confessions of a Millionaire's Mistress* as Celeste and Ben find they want the same thing in the bedroom…but different things from life! Plus, look out for Nicola Marsh's *The Boss's Bedroom Agenda,* in which a sizzling night spent together between Beth and her gorgeous new boss, Aidan, changes everything!

We'd love to hear what you think about Harlequin Presents. E-mail us at Presents@hmb.co.uk, or join in the discussions at www.iheartpresents.com and www.sensationalromance.blogspot.com, where you'll also find more information about books and authors!

Even if at times work is rather boring,
there is one person making the office a whole
lot more interesting: the boss!

Dark and dangerous, alpha and powerful,
rich and ruthless… He's in control, he knows
what he wants and he's going to get it!
He's tall, handsome and breathtakingly attractive.
And there's one outcome that's never in doubt—
the heroines of these supersexy
stories will be:

From sensible suits...into satin sheets!

A brand-new miniseries only available from
Harlequin Presents!

Nicola Marsh

THE BOSS'S BEDROOM AGENDA

Undressed
BY THE BOSS

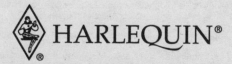

HARLEQUIN®

TORONTO • NEW YORK • LONDON
AMSTERDAM • PARIS • SYDNEY • HAMBURG
STOCKHOLM • ATHENS • TOKYO • MILAN • MADRID
PRAGUE • WARSAW • BUDAPEST • AUCKLAND

Recycling programs
for this product may
not exist in your area.

ISBN-13: 978-0-373-12802-0
ISBN-10:   0-373-12802-9

THE BOSS'S BEDROOM AGENDA

First North American Publication 2009.

Copyright © 2008 by Nicola Marsh.

www.eHarlequin.com

Printed in U.S.A.

All about the author...
Nicola Marsh

NICOLA MARSH has always had a passion for writing and reading. As a youngster, she devoured books when she should have been sleeping, and later she kept a diary, whose content could be an epic in itself! These days, she's either enjoying life with her husband and son in her home city of Melbourne, or at her computer, creating the romances she loves, in her dream job.

Visit Nicola's Web site at www.nicolamarsh.com for the latest news of her books.

For my blog readers, who cheered me on
with this one every step of the way.
Thank you, you're the best!

CHAPTER ONE

BETHANY WALKER stuck her tongue out at her reflection as she twirled in front of the floor-length mirror.

'I look gross.'

Her cousin Lana smirked. 'I officially pronounce you a bona fide nerd.'

'I do look like a nerd, don't I?'

Lana, queen of the nerds and loving it, pushed her tortoise-shell glasses further up her nose as her serious gaze travelled from the tips of Beth's low-heeled black pumps to the top of her blonde hair pulled back in a tight bun.

'You look exactly how a proper tour guide should. You'll fit in at the museum, no worries.'

Beth screwed up her nose as she smoothed the stiff cotton of her ultra-plain white blouse. 'How could you wear such hideous clothes?'

Lana quirked an eyebrow and picked up Beth's discarded apple-green midriff top and cut-off denim shorts from the floor. 'I could ask you the same question.'

'Touché, cuz. Touché.'

Beth grinned, eternally grateful for the close relationship she shared with her cousin.

From the first moment Lana had stood up to her, a mousy

six-year-old who refused to back down when the boisterous, pushy pain in the butt she used to be had tried to wrestle a doll out of her hands, their friendship had been cemented.

'Anything else you want me to cram before I do this? Any last minute pep talk? Instructions? Ways to bore the entire city of Melbourne senseless as they troop through the museum?'

The corners of Lana's mouth twitched. 'There is one more thing.'

'What?'

She didn't like the gleam in her cousin's eye, the one that screamed she wasn't done turning a swan into an ugly duckling just yet.

'Here.' Lana opened the top drawer of her dresser and reached into the back. 'You need to wear these to complete the look.'

Her heart sank as she saw the ugliest pair of glasses she'd ever laid eyes on resting on her cousin's outstretched palm.

Shaking her head, she held up her hands in protest. 'Uh-uh. No way. Haven't I done enough? You've dressed me, prepped me, turned me into another you. You can't make me wear those!'

Lana cracked up. 'I know, I'm just kidding around. Though I hear these are the latest fashion statement for all the cool tour guides this year.'

'I bet.'

Beth rolled her eyes, grimacing at the ugly black-rimmed glasses, ignoring the faintest ring of 'four eyes, four eyes' in her ears.

If she'd hated being a brain as a kid she'd hated wearing glasses more and the memories had lasted way too long; long enough until she'd got a part-time job and earned enough money to buy contacts at the age of sixteen.

As for the old saying 'guys didn't make passes at girls who wore glasses' it had been all too true in her case and she'd set about correcting that impression the second those contacts slipped in. She'd transformed from shy geek to flirty femme fatale and hadn't looked back.

'You sure? It would complete your new look.'

Lana stood back, folded her arms and admired her handiwork while Beth felt like the bride of Frankenstein in her ugly shoes and uglier clothes.

'You know I'm not really going to wear this get-up, don't you? I'm merely doing this to humour you?'

'Yeah, I know. You'll probably rock up to the museum in a micro mini and halter top, right?'

'Now that you mention it…'

Lana groaned. 'Tell me again why I helped set up the interview for you.'

Beth patted her arm as she shimmied out of her cousin's clothes and slipped back into her own, rehanging the awful suit and slamming the wardrobe door shut before she had to look at it for another second. 'Because you think I'm the bee's knees. Because blood is thicker than water. And any other soppy cliché you can think of.'

Lana's mouth twitched, her patient expression one Beth had seen many times before. 'So what are you really wearing?'

The image of her new David Lawrence raven pinstripe suit with the fabulous pencil skirt complete with flirty frill flashed across her mind and she did a little jig complete with arm twirl and cancan leg kicks.

'I've bought a gorgeous suit. *Me*, in a *suit*. Can you believe it?'

Lana chuckled. 'Actually, no, I can't. This I have to see.'

'I'll drop by on my way home so you can check it out. Speaking of which…' she glanced at her watch and grimaced '…I better hit the road.'

'Yeah, you're pushing for time. You should get going.' Lana took a hop towards the door and a ripple of pain flashed across her face.

'Hey, you need to sit down. That ankle isn't going to heal if you don't take it easy. And as much as I appreciate your help in telling me about the vacancy for this job, it isn't going to be the same traipsing around that mausoleum without you.'

Lana's presence would've made her induction into monotonous regular work bearable. Given a choice she would rather be holed up in her warehouse apartment creating the metal sculptures she loved, but she needed this job desperately and while acting as tour guide at Melbourne Museum wouldn't set her world on fire, it would take her one step closer to her dream.

'God, you're pushy.'

Lana slipped the crutches back under her armpits and hopped to a hard-backed chair a few steps away before sinking onto it with a barely suppressed groan. 'And I'll be back on deck just as soon as this damn ankle heals.'

She winced as she lifted her leg beneath the knee and propped the ankle on a pouffe. 'I'm sorry I won't be there to show you the ropes like I promised. I know this isn't your ideal job and I said I'd help ease you into it…until this!' She pointed at her plaster cast and scowled.

'Don't worry, cuz. All I have to do is remember the stuff we swotted and take a bunch of curious geeks around the museum. Easy.'

Lana didn't look convinced.

'You've heard about the new boss? He's the son of the old CEO and a major player in archaeological circles so, while Abe Voss hired you, I have no idea how tough Aidan is.'

Beth plopped on a nearby footstool and gently patted the

cast. 'I'll have to smile my way into his good books. I'm sure this new boss won't be any different.'

'So you think you can charm him, huh?'

By the dubious expression on Lana's face, she could see what her competent, super-intelligent, serious older cousin thought of that.

'Either that or dazzle him with my tour-guide skills, one or the other. Come on, you know you can trust me to do a brilliant job and keep the Walker girls' prize-employee reputations intact, right?'

Lana chuckled and rolled her eyes. 'Do you really want me to answer that?'

'Actually, no.'

They laughed in unison, remembering the countless times Beth had asked Lana to trust her only to stand her up in favour of a boy, a cool party or the latest fashion sale.

'You'll be fine. If you have any questions during the day, you can always sneak into the Ladies and buzz me on your mobile.'

'Hmm…real professional.' Beth grinned, bounced up and slung her designer bag over her shoulder. 'Right. Time to strut my stuff.'

'Okay, off you go. And remember—don't do anything I wouldn't do.'

'Yes, m'am.' She saluted, sending Lana's ankle a pointed look. 'Aren't you going to wish me luck? Something along the lines of "break a leg"?'

Lana pointed towards the door. 'Out. And take your lousy sense of humour with you.'

Beth pouted and stuck a hand on a hip. 'Now is that any way to talk to the museum's new star tour guide?'

Lana quirked a bushy eyebrow in desperate need of a good plucking. 'Star, huh? I'd be happy with good, sensible, dedicated tour guide. You know, the type of tour guide who does a great job and impresses the new boss so much he can't wait for his new star curator to start.'

'Sensible? Mmm...' Beth grinned, yanked down her funky top and did a little shimmy in her tight denim mini. 'Don't worry, cuz. You can count on me.'

She only just heard Lana's murmured, 'That's what I'm afraid of,' as she strolled out the door with a spring in her step.

'These shoes are something else,' Beth murmured, staring down at her new Sonia Rykiel satin-toed sable pumps with delight.

She really should've worn something more comfortable for her first day on the job, yet considering she was currently squashed on a peak-hour tram between a sweaty businessman and a scruffy uni student who hadn't discovered the joys of deodorant yet, the snazzy new shoes were a comfort.

She'd dithered over a pair of sexy sling-backs, wishing she could slip into a comfy pair of inappropriate fancy flip-flops, before settling on the pumps with a killer heel and just the right amount of beaded detail around the forefoot.

She was a devoted shoe girl, always choosing the perfect shoe to suit her mood, and right now these new pumps gave her a much-needed confidence boost.

Traipsing around a museum all day rather than sculpting her precious metal hadn't been high on her priority list until recently, but with the bank breathing down her neck she needed a steady job and this was it.

Sighing, she hugged her tote bag tighter to her chest, somewhat comforted by the stab of stilettos through the soft leather. She had a date with an old uni buddy after work and after calling at Lana's as promised, she wouldn't have time to head home to change so had brought her outfit with her.

The simple knowledge she had another pair of fabulous shoes in her bag made her feel a whole lot better.

Unfortunately, she didn't feel comforted for long. As the tram screeched to a stop outside the museum, she stepped off and took two steps before a heel caught in the tracks and stuck there. It wouldn't have been a problem if she'd stuck too. However, with a quick glance at her watch sending her scurrying, her body weight pitched forward while the heel didn't and it broke with a resounding snap.

She muttered a few unladylike curses Lana would never approve of as she stared at the beautiful heel sticking out of the tracks.

Great, not only had she ruined a pair of sensational new shoes, but she'd be starting a few minutes late—without a pair of shoes!

As if reminding her of their presence, a stiletto dug into her ribs as she tucked her bag under her arm and she perked up, grabbed the offending heel out of the tracks, dashed across the road and plopped onto a wrought-iron bench.

Fishing her favourite Manolos out of the bag, she slipped off the pumps and wriggled her fuchsia-painted toes into the sandals, sighing at the luxurious feel of her favourite shoes adorning her feet.

Pushing aside the thought that sexy black patent sandals with tiny straps and decorated with feathers probably weren't appropriate tour-guide footwear, she strode towards the museum as fast as her three-inch stilettos could carry her.

With the correct footwear, a girl could face anything and right then Beth knew her day was looking up.

Those shoes are something else, Aidan Voss thought as he caught sight of the new tour guide sashaying across the polished marble floor towards him, her nose in the air and a small smile playing about her glossed lips.

She looked as if she didn't have a care in the world rather than a woman who was five minutes late her first day on the job.

'Miss Walker?'

'Yes?'

If her shoes were something else, her dazzling green eyes captured his attention and shot it into the stratosphere. They sparkled with intelligence, and even a hint of wariness couldn't hide the glint of fun in their rich moss-green depths.

'You're late,' he said, his gaze roaming over her heart-shaped face with the high cheekbones, pert nose and lush mouth a tad on the full side.

Her features should've clashed. Instead, they melded into a heart-stopping combination and, for a guy who appreciated beautiful things on a daily basis and had since he could first walk and talk, he couldn't tear his gaze away.

'And you are?'

Surprised by her assured comeback when she should've been on the back foot, and more than a little annoyed at his urge to laugh, he said, 'Someone who could have your butt for waltzing in here late on your first day.'

If her confidence surprised him, her glossed lips curving into a saucy smile shocked the hell out of him.

'You could have my butt, huh? Sounds like an interesting way to foster employee relations.'

His mouth twitched despite the urge to send her packing before she'd begun.

From scanning her CV he'd expected an eager-to-learn, deferent trainee. Instead, with her sun-streaked blonde hair perched high on her head in a jaunty pony-tail, a figure-hugging pinstripe suit outlining a compact, curvaceous body and a pale pink shirt that reminded him of freshly spun candy floss, this woman screamed 'sex kitten' rather than tour guide.

Sex kitten? Where had that come from?

Dropping his gaze to her feet and those funky shoes, he knew exactly what had put the idea into his head.

He was a leg man through and through, and the sight of her curvy stockingless calves and dainty feet thrust into shoes that definitely didn't belong to a conservative tour guide had his head in a spin.

He chose to ignore her sassy remark, considering his obsession with her legs didn't need the added burden of thinking about her butt too.

'I'm not an employee.'

He sent her his best glower, the one that made most workers jump to his tune on various digs around the world.

Her eyes lit up, sparking green fire as she tilted her chin up. 'In that case, you have no right telling me off. So if you don't mind—'

'I'm your *employer.*'

He expected to see fear or the glimmer of an apology replacing the glint in her eyes.

Once again, she proved him wrong.

'Pleased to meet you. Beth Walker, tour guide extraordinaire at your service.'

She stuck out her hand, a wide grin curving her lips and he found himself unwittingly returning her smile while he shook her hand.

'Aidan Voss, the new boss around here.'

A boss who had no right noticing how her eyes twinkled when she smiled or the cheeky lilt in her voice when she spoke, as if challenging him to do goodness knew what.

'Do you personally greet all your employees?'

'Only the ones who are late on their first day.' He tapped his watch face. 'I must say your lack of punctuality surprises me, Miss Walker.'

'Call me Beth.' She dropped her gaze, but not before he'd seen a flicker of fear, the first sign she was anything other than confident. 'And I'm really sorry for being late. I was running on time until I had a shoe crisis.'

Once again, his lips gave a decided twitch and he clamped down his urge to laugh out loud.

'Speaking of your shoes, do you think they're appropriate for your role here?'

She gripped her bag tighter, her knuckles standing out, as he glimpsed another sign Beth 'Fancy Feet' Walker might be more rattled than she let on.

'Shoes this good are always appropriate…' She trailed off as he frowned at her and her fingers flexed around the strap of her leather carry-all again. 'Considering I broke a heel on my pumps in the tram tracks out front a few minutes ago, I had no choice. It's my Manolos or go without and I'd hazard a guess you wouldn't go for the bare look?'

Finding his gaze drawn unwittingly to those sexy shoes again, he wrenched it upward with effort, determinedly ignoring how great she'd probably look padding around these hallowed halls barefoot.

Clearing his throat, he said, 'Just make sure you wear something more appropriate tomorrow.'

Her lips curved in a tentative smile. 'So that means I'm not in too much trouble for being five minutes late?'

'Don't push your luck,' he muttered, intrigued by the contrasting combination of confident woman one moment, vulnerable new employee the next.

Even now, while her fidgeting fingers toying with her bag strap belied her nerves, she met his gaze without the slightest hint of intimidation.

He'd never met anyone like her, most of the people he worked with deferring to his experience or in awe of his connections in the archaeological world.

As a new employee, she would know about his family and their role in the museum yet she acted as if he were an acquaintance. Or, worse, as if he were a guy she could flirt with.

'If there's nothing else, I'll get started?'

Nodding, he tried another frown for good measure. It had little effect as a sunny smile banished the last hint of any susceptibility and transformed her into cheeky ingénue in a heartbeat.

'Fine. I take it you had your tour following the interview?'

'Uh-huh.'

'Then you can start in the Australia Gallery today. It should be quiet in there as we're not expecting many school groups and Mondays are notoriously flat around here anyway. Any questions?'

'No, thanks. I'm ready and raring to go.'

He blinked, struck by how every word tumbling out of her lush mouth sounded like a naughty invitation.

Annoyed at his wayward thoughts, especially in relation to an employee, and hating how she'd had him on the back foot since he'd first laid eyes on her, he injected the right amount of coolness into his voice. 'That's all for now. Good luck.'

Her confident smile didn't waver. 'Thanks, but I don't need it. I'm good at what I do.'

With that, she turned on those ridiculous three-inch heels and strutted away—in the wrong direction.

'Beth, the Australia Gallery is that way.'

She stiffened and paused mid-step, swinging back to face him, and he pointed over his right shoulder.

Something akin to panic flickered in her eyes for a second, though it could've been a trick of the light as the bright sun's rays of a Melbourne spring morning filtered through the towering glass comprising the museum's shell.

'I knew that.'

She fidgeted with the strap on her bag, sending him a tight smile at total odds with her previous self-assurance. 'I was hoping for a quick caffeine fix before I started.'

'The staff cafeteria's that way too.'

He grinned, somewhat satisfied to see her flustered as she gripped her bag tighter.

With a dismissive shrug, she set off in the opposite direction. 'I've always had a lousy sense of direction.'

'Well, I expect you to get up to speed pretty quick around here. After all, how do you expect to take tours if you need a map and a compass yourself?'

'I'll be fine.' Some of her earlier pluck returned as she tilted her chin in the air to send him a glare. 'Thanks for the welcome, but it's time I started my new job.'

He couldn't help but smile at her confidence, eager to return to his office and check out her résumé again.

Either his father was losing his touch at reading people or there was a lot more to their newest tour guide than met the eye.

'I hear the boss is a compulsive clock-watcher.'

With that parting comment she waltzed away, looking way too appealing in that snazzy suit, the tight skirt with a little flare grazing her knees leaving him with an unimpeded view of those sensational legs.

Oh, yeah, he definitely needed to read up on his newest employee.

Anyone who could wear shoes like that on her first day and not be intimidated by him was worth watching and he had every intention of keeping a close eye on her.

Very close.

CHAPTER TWO

'COULD this place *be* any bigger?'

Beth muttered under her breath, scanning the endless corridor for a sign of the Australia Gallery.

She'd been the length and breadth of the rabbit warren of corridors, following the clearly marked signs, but had somehow ended up in the dinosaur room, the creepy crawly room and the reptile room without a glimmer of Australiana in sight.

'Can I help you?'

Beth inwardly groaned. Just what she needed, someone else pulling her up for being late or lost when she should know her way around here.

Fixing a smile on her face, she turned towards the tentative voice. 'Actually, you can. This is my first day on the job and I was a bit frazzled after the interview when I got the grand tour and can't seem to find the Australia Gallery.'

The young woman's bemused expression spoke volumes. She obviously thought the new tour guide was a brainless bimbo.

'I'm heading that way myself.'

'Great.'

She fell into step with the woman whose name badge had 'Dorothy' typed in bold black print as she surreptitiously checked out Dorothy's footwear for signs of sparkly red shoes—and was not in the least surprised when she found staid black flats instead.

'I'm Beth, by the way.'

'Dorothy. I'm a volunteer.'

'You don't get paid to be here?'

Jeez, she could think of any place she'd rather be if she wasn't doing this for the stability factor. Steady job plus adequate funds equalled a lease on a small gallery to showcase her work and right now she needed that lease. She'd waited long enough to set her dream in motion.

'I'm an archaeology student. I do this for a bit of extra experience.' Dorothy's brown eyes lit up for a moment, brightening her make-up-less face.

'You must really love what you do.'

Dorothy nodded, her bobbing head setting her bun wobbling precariously atop her head. 'And the opportunity to work alongside someone of Aidan Voss's calibre was too good to pass up.'

Beth's ears pricked up. She'd been so busy trying to find her way around this maze she'd deliberately pushed aside thoughts of her boss.

Guys who looked like Aidan Voss didn't enter her sphere too often. The proverbial tall, dark and handsome seemed way too trite when describing his devastating looks. If it hadn't been for the inch-long scar near his right eyebrow, he could've modelled rather than dig around old ruins and keep watch for recalcitrant tour guides.

'So he's good?'

Beth kept her tone casual despite the sudden urge to learn more about the guy with the sharp cheekbones, strong jaw, slate-grey eyes and hint of a dimple. Not that she'd memorised every detail of that striking face or anything.

Dorothy's incredulous expression had Beth biting the inside of her cheek to prevent laughing out loud.

'Good? He's the best. Not only does he come from one of the most renowned historian families in Australia, he's been responsible for several major finds around the world. Egypt, South America, Greece, you name it, he's done it.'

A faint blush stained Dorothy's pale cheeks and Beth had a feeling the boss's good looks hadn't gone completely un-noticed by the enthusiastic volunteer.

'But surely you know all this? I would've thought the lure of working with a man like Mr Voss would be irresistible to anyone interested in this business?'

'Oh, working with Mr Voss is irresistible all right.'

Beth's memory worked down from that chiseled face to the way he'd filled out his charcoal suit, how his powder-blue business shirt had stretched taut across his chest and how he'd strutted rather than walked.

In those few minutes he'd hauled her up for being tardy she'd had the impression of a self-assured guy, a guy on top of his game, a guy who could turn a girl's head without trying.

Not that he was her type. She preferred her men scruffier, less domineering, more casual, and the super-confident Aidan Voss definitely didn't fit that bill.

Not that she should even consider him as any 'type'. Lana would keel over and break her other ankle if she thought for one second Beth was sizing up their boss as 'sexy guy' material.

'Well, here we are.'

'Thanks,' Beth said, momentarily distracted by thoughts of Aidan as sexy and pulling up just in time to stop slamming into Dorothy's ramrod-straight back.

'I'll be fine from here,' she added, eager to get rid of the volunteer so she could start doing some serious exploring and familiarise herself with the room. Though she'd studied up on the museum and done some serious swotting with Lana, she couldn't afford to make any more gaffs. Her job depended on it and, in turn, her ticket out of here and into her dream gallery.

Dorothy hesitated, toying with her name badge while a small frown creased her brow. 'Can I ask you something?'

'Sure.' Beth hoped it wasn't a question about Phar Lap's location or where the authentic *Neighbours* set was.

'Where did you get those amazing shoes?'

She laughed and wriggled her toes, still rueing her broken satin-toed pumps but delighting in her Manolos.

'I'm hopeless with fashion and I'd kill to have a pair like that.'

Feeling decidedly like Professor Henry Higgins in *My Fair Lady* about to make over Eliza Doolittle, Beth said, 'Why don't we meet for lunch and I'll let you in on all the best shoe shops in Melbourne?'

'Great. See you in the cafeteria at one.'

Dorothy's genuine smile was the first hint of real warmth she'd seen in the rather plain girl and as she watched her walk away in her brown trousers and matching jacket, with a prim cream blouse, severe hairstyle and not a skerrick of style, Beth definitely felt like the professor about to make a grand magnanimous gesture.

It wasn't till she entered the room, her eyes assaulted by myriad displays that made her dizzy, did she realise she'd made a mistake.

She should be focussing on getting up to scratch in here, not indulging her passion for retail therapy. This job was too important and she'd already made a less than favourable impression with her lateness.

Sighing, she shook her head and headed for the first

display. This business of being a *good, sensible, dedicated* tour guide was going to be a lot harder than she'd thought.

Aidan sat back in his oversized leather chair and stared out of the wide window at the Royal Exhibition Building framed by a cloudless blue sky.

He loved the old building, had loved this view the first moment he'd entered his dad's office as a cocky archaeological student determined to take on the world. Or, more correctly, travel the world in search of the ancient relics that made his pulse pound with excitement and always had since he'd accompanied his parents on his first dig as an inquisitive five-year-old.

He'd never forgotten the feel of hot sand beneath his hands as he'd dug alongside them with a miniature spade, the heat of an unforgiving Egyptian sun beating down as he'd scrabbled harder and harder until he'd found the small mummy figurine his father had assured him was there.

It wasn't till years later he'd realised his dad had planted it there for him to find, but by then he'd chosen his path. He'd wanted to be an archaeologist, the best in the business. His dad might have chosen a desk job despite being the top historian in Australia, but he'd wanted more, had craved more.

Rather ironic, considering he now sat in his dad's vacated chair, the last place he wanted to be.

Grabbing the phone, he punched number one on speed dial, knowing his dad would berate him for interrupting his siesta, remembering times gone by when the indefatigable Abe Voss would've been out and about at this time of the morning, prime exploratory time before the scorching outback sun sent even the hardiest explorer scurrying for shade.

'Abraham Voss speaking.'

Abe's clipped tones elicited a wry grin. Aidan had never

known the old man to answer the phone any other way, especially when he had more important things to do with his time.

'Hey, Dad, it's me.'

'What's up?'

Aidan stiffened, Abe's gruff, brisk tone the same abrasive way he'd spoken to him all his life, as if he were an interruption to be tolerated.

No niceties, no normal exchange of pleasantries. But then, what did he expect—for him to change just because he was doing the old man a favour?

Swallowing his annoyance, he swivelled his chair away from the view and picked up Beth Walker's résumé.

'I met the new tour guide this morning. She's not what I expected.'

'She's something else, isn't she? I knew she'd be perfect for the job.'

'Something else' was right. The minute he'd laid eyes on Beth Walker he'd known she was perfect—though, inappropriately, work had been the furthest thing from his mind.

Frowning, he tapped her résumé against the desk. 'Her credentials aren't super impressive. Tour guide at Flemington during the Spring Racing Carnival and at the Melbourne Grand Prix isn't exactly the same as here, is it?'

'Are you questioning my judgement?'

Hell, yeah.

But he wouldn't push it. The only reason he was sitting in this chair was because his father had asked him to, had made the first overture in his life to acknowledge his skills, and he wasn't about to sabotage the tentative professional mateship they'd developed lately.

'Guess her demeanour threw me a little.'

'Why? Because she's a tad on the exuberant side?' Abe

snorted, an exasperated sound that told him exactly what he thought of this phone call. 'Look, Lana Walker will be a huge credit to the museum. She's the best curator on the eastern seaboard and I trusted her judgement when she recommended her cousin. Then I interviewed Beth and she's exactly the type of employee we need. Fresh, vibrant, willing to learn. So what's the problem?'

'No problem.'

Not unless he counted the awful sinking feeling he was attracted to her when he shouldn't be.

CEOs shouldn't fraternise with staff, even ones with sparkling eyes, cheeky smiles, flamboyant suits and come-get-me shoes.

'If that's all, I have to go. Your mother has me on this crazy exercise regimen.'

Aidan paused, knowing Abe hated talking about his health, well aware he'd irritated the old man enough for one day with his interrogation about Beth.

'How's the heart?'

'Fine. Blood pressure's down. No angina since we came up here.'

'Great—'

'Must go. I'll call you next week to check up on how the place is doing.'

The dial tone hummed in his ear before he'd had a chance to say goodbye and Aidan snapped his mobile shut, the familiar disappointment clawing at him.

The old man would never change and he'd be a fool to hope otherwise. Yet when Abe had been advised by the docs to rest up or risk a heart attack and he'd made the decision to head for the tropics of Queensland for a little R & R, he'd turned straight to his son.

Aidan hadn't been able to refuse, buoyed by the uncharacteristic action of a man who'd barely acknowledged his achievements growing up, a small part of him still hoping for the unthinkable to happen, that dear old Dad would finally recognise his worth.

So here he was, trying to prove a point, aiming to be the best damn CEO the museum had ever seen even if it was only for a few months.

He'd made that more than clear. There was no way he'd give up his passion for the digs.

He'd made that mistake once before.

Never again.

Being the best CEO meant keeping a close eye on employees… Scanning Beth's résumé again, he shook his head.

His gut instinct had served him well in the past, giving him a feel for the best sites to search, directing him where to dig.

Maybe in this case his instincts were wrong?

However, the more he read of Beth's résumé and her apparent lack of skills, and compared it with the mental image he had of the feisty tour guide, the more he had the feeling she wasn't the right person for the job.

But he believed in giving people a fair go so that was exactly what he'd do here. However, if the cutesy tour guide made one too many mistakes… He shoved her résumé back into its folder and stood up.

He wanted this place running up to speed and the only way to ensure that was to do spot checks on his staff.

Starting with one highly unusual tour guide.

CHAPTER THREE

'So how did it go?'

Beth took a long, drawn-out sip of her mocha-mint iced latte and smacked her lips, trying to hide a grin at Lana's anxious expression and failing.

'This isn't funny, Beth. I'm in agony over here and I'm not just talking about my ankle!'

'Okay, okay, hang on to your crutches.'

She drained the rest of her favourite drink, placed the take-out cup on the coffee table and stretched. 'There isn't much to tell. My first day was uneventful and glitch-free.'

Well, almost, if she didn't count her run-in with the charismatic Aidan Voss first thing in the morning and the slight mishap with the train display later.

Lana frowned and gave her the same disgusted look she reserved just for her ever since they'd been playmates fighting over the same crayons or dolls.

'Right. Now tell me the truth. All of it.'

Beth blew her cousin a raspberry.

'Where do you want me to start? The part where I broke my heel on the way in and got into trouble with the boss? Or the part where I got lost traipsing around that monstrosity?

Or the part where I befriended this lovely volunteer in desperate need of a fashion makeover and took her shopping?'

Lana guffawed. 'So I guess you couldn't charm or smile your way out of everything, huh?'

'Hey, it's only my first day. Give a girl a chance to work her magic.'

Lana rolled her eyes. 'Now that we've established your indefatigable self-confidence hasn't taken a beating, tell me exactly what happened.'

Beth waved a hand in the air and reached for a melt-in-the-mouth Brunetti's biscotti with the other. 'Teething problems, cuz. Everyone has them in a new job.'

'I know, but I'm bored out of my brain here all day, wondering what's going on over at the museum.' She slapped her injured leg and grimaced. 'I hate being this helpless, this dependent on other people.'

'You mean me?'

Lana had an independent streak a mile long. Guess it came with the territory of losing her mum early. In a way, her cousin's tragedy had bonded them as nothing else would. Considering she'd lost her own mum in the same car accident the two of them had clung to each other, a pair of devastated six-year-olds with their worlds turned upside down. And hers had never righted.

'I know you're doing your best.' Lana's grim expression implied her best wasn't good enough. 'It's just that I don't think I can last three months sitting around here doing nothing but paperwork.'

'You don't exactly have a choice.'

A bit like herself, actually. She owed Lana and if her cousin had asked her to walk on water she would have. Trying her best not to slip up while working at the museum was small payback for everything her cousin had done for her. Not to mention the added bonus of the fact she really needed this job!

Her muse had gone AWOL along with her latest boyfriend, taking her chance of having a display in his gallery along with him. Though she should be grateful: the rat's actions had prompted her to finally follow her dream and lease her own space. If the powers that be at the stuffy bank ever gave her the loan to secure it, that was.

Renting her warehouse and spending most of her earnings on fashion and shoes didn't build a great credit rating and, boy, had the bank bigwigs rubbed her nose in it.

'Good point. So tell me about the boss. What's Aidan Voss like? I've heard on the grapevine he's a gun.'

Son of a gun, more like it, Beth thought, remembering those slate-grey eyes and their calculating expression as they sized her up.

'He's quite impressive.'

An unexpected quiver of excitement skittered down her spine as she contemplated exactly how impressive Aidan Voss was.

'His credentials, you mean?'

'I mean the whole package.'

Oops. Beth mentally slapped herself for putting together 'impressive' and 'package' in her imaginative mind.

A furrow appeared on her cousin's brow. 'I don't like that gleam in your eye.'

'What gleam?'

She tried her best innocent look and knew it came up lacking when Lana groaned and shook her head.

'The gleam you get whenever any male under thirty-five and halfway good-looking enters your world.'

Tilting her nose in the air as if she didn't give a damn, Beth said, 'I have no idea of his age. From how tense he appears he's probably ancient.'

'And the good-looking part?'

Trust Lana not to back down. Damn it, she was like a dog with the proverbial bone. Or in this case, the curator with a dinosaur bone.

'He's not bad for an uptight older dude who likes fossicking for boring old artefacts.'

Lana laughed, the sound echoing around her quaint single-storey weatherboard in one of Carlton's quieter streets.

'I'm on to you.' Lana's laugh grew to belly-shaking proportions. 'Your version of not bad equates with sex god. So he's that good?'

Beth nodded, joining in the laughter. 'Better. Honestly, you should see this guy. Tall, great bod, killer smile, fabulous eyes. A knockout.'

'Don't forget the brain behind the *package*.'

Lana's not-so-subtle emphasis on the last word had them in fits.

'You'll see him soon enough.'

'If I don't hack this leg off in frustration over the next few months, that is.'

Her cousin's laughter petered out so Beth did the only thing possible, the one thing she'd done her whole life to cope when faced with uncomfortable circumstances; made light of the situation.

'And miss out on seeing Voss the Boss in the flesh? Not likely.'

Lana cringed. 'You know you just called one of the most influential men in archaeological circles Voss the Boss? Just make sure that little gem stays between us.'

'You got it.' She leaned forward, tapped the side of her

nose and dropped her voice to a conspiratorial whisper. 'Now, would you like me to bat my eyelashes at him to get on his good side? You know, to keep the Walker girls in favour with the boss.'

'Don't you dare!'

Lana's eyes widened in horror behind her tortoiseshell glasses and Beth chuckled.

'Don't worry, cuz. I have no intention of flirting with the boss.'

However, she had to resist the urge to squirm under her cousin's speculative glance as she quickly pushed aside the thought she already had.

Beth ignored the wolf-whistle of a passer-by as she strolled down Lygon Street on her way to meet Bobby, her friend— and date for the evening.

Not that catching up for a drink with Bobby was a date exactly. In fact, the thought of seeing the lanky, red-headed drummer as anything other than friend material brought a smile to her face.

So she'd dressed up? No big deal. She'd needed to slip into her favourite black mini and shimmery aubergine top to feel halfway normal again after spending all day in a suit, stylish as it was.

As she passed her favourite gelateria and studiously avoided looking in the window to stop from drooling all over her top, her mobile rang and she scrambled in her bag, hoping Bobby wasn't standing her up. She was really looking forward to a drink, some light-hearted conversation and the inevitable laughs that spending an evening with a good mate entailed.

It had been way too long since she'd had a good night out; she, the party girl of Melbourne, had spent too many evenings lately holed up in Lana's place, swotting up on the museum. Bor-ing. Time to live a little, just as she used to.

Staring at the caller ID and not recognising the number, she hit the answer button. 'Beth Walker.'

'Hello, Beth. Aidan Voss here.'

She stumbled and would've sprawled onto the nearest café table if a kind waiter, with the deepest chocolate-brown eyes she'd ever seen, hadn't reached out to steady her.

Mouthing 'thanks' at the waiter, whose wink had her beaming back at him, she continued walking while furiously trying to think up something fabulously witty to say, anything other than, 'What do you want?'

'Sorry to ring you after hours but I need to see you.'

Great, he needed to see her. Some first impression she must've made.

Unbidden, the memory of the way he'd looked at her that morning sprung to mind and she wondered if the sizzle of something between them wasn't just a figment of her imagination.

'I can come in early first thing tomorrow,' she said, banishing her ludicrous thoughts and trying to keep her tone businesslike.

'I need to see you now.'

'Oh.'

Damn, that one tiny syllable came out on a sigh and she quickly reassembled her wits.

'Sorry, no can do. I have other plans.'

'This isn't a request, it's an order.'

His silky-smooth voice did little to disguise the thread of steel beneath. Here was a guy used to making people jump, people who probably asked how high.

'I'm meeting someone,' she blurted, gnawing at her bottom lip the instant the words left her mouth, realising how stupid it sounded as an excuse. As if high and mighty Aidan Voss would care if she had a date or not.

'Far be it from me to disrupt your love life, but this is important and it can't wait till morning.'

'Bobby's just an old friend,' she said, refraining from slapping her head, just, as another corker popped out of her mouth without her thinking.

Damn it, what was it about this guy that rattled her so much? She usually handled guys with finesse, flirting with them while keeping them at arm's length, using quips and witty repartee rather than blurting the first thing that came into her head.

'I'm glad.'

He paused and for one insane second she hoped he might be glad she wasn't on a real date—before realising why the heck would he care? She was just an employee, a lousy one at that if his unimpressed tone and his order to see her immediately was any indication.

'That means you can take a rain check and Bobby won't be disappointed. I'll meet you in the museum foyer in an hour.'

Cupping her hand over the phone, Beth sighed. She was so tempted to tell him where to get off, but the bank needed proof of a reputable job before considering her application for a loan to secure the gallery's five-year lease, so she had no option but to do what he wanted.

Removing her hand, she said, 'Fine. I'll be there. Though the least you can do is tell me what this is all about.'

'That episode with the train display today? The child's mother has lodged an incident report and we need to discuss it.'

Incident report? Great, just great. As a first day on the job this one sucked, big time.

Clamping down on the flicker of fear that this pending

meeting couldn't be good for her job security, she mustered her best contrite tone. 'No problems. See you in an hour.'

'One other thing.'

'What is it?'

'Don't be late.'

He hung up before she could respond and with a resigned sigh she snapped the phone shut and flung it into her bag.

If it weren't for Lana and her dream gallery at stake, she would walk away from this less-than-appealing situation and never look back.

She wasn't a tour guide, she was an artist, and having to follow someone else's rules didn't sit well with her. She was used to creative freedom, to being her own boss, not jumping to someone else's tune.

As she passed a bright, airy shopfront filled with exquisite paintings and sculptures she sucked in a deep breath and squared her shoulders.

She wanted that.

Her very own space filled with *her* work, with the autonomy to do what she wanted when she wanted. Recognition for her talents, recognition of any sort if she were completely honest with herself, something she'd craved from her dad and never got considering he'd spent the bulk of her childhood traipsing around the countryside.

Casting one last longing glance at the mini-gallery, she tucked her bag tighter and picked up the pace.

She could do this.

She had a job to do and she'd better do it well.

Achieving her dream depended on it.

Aidan paced the empty entrance hall of the museum and wondered what the hell he was doing.

He'd had a very bad day, starting with a pile of boring financial reports and ending in a complaint from an irate mother.

Though officially his day hadn't been all bad and it hadn't exactly started off with those reports considering he'd laid down the law to the new tour guide first thing.

Ironic, he'd be ending his day the same way he'd started: glancing at his watch and shaking his head at Beth Walker's lack of punctuality.

He shouldn't even be here.

Confronting her over the train-display drama could've waited till morning, but something had prompted him to ring and order her back tonight.

He muttered a curse, knowing exactly what that 'something' was: fascination.

She had him wound up tighter than a DNA strand and he needed to see her now for no other reason than to reassure himself that his absorption with her when he should've been focussing on those reports had stemmed from interest in the skills of a new employee and not an underlying fatalistic attraction he couldn't act upon.

As if on cue a loud tapping sounded on the glass door in front of him and he flicked the lock, sliding a finger between his collar and neck while doing so.

He needed some air, fast.

His lungs had seized the second he laid eyes on Beth in a shimmery purple top, full make-up, blonde hair sleek and a black mini skirt that would keep him up all night.

Correction, the memory of her long, tanned legs on full display in that skirt would do that.

'Let me guess. You're going to tell me off for being a few minutes late.'

The full megawattage of her smile hit him as she flicked

her hair over her shoulder in a gesture suggesting habit rather than an attempt to capture his attention.

Not that she needed to do anything other than stand there to do that.

'I saw you staring at your watch just before I knocked.'

'Occupational habit.' He ushered her in and locked the door, trying not to inhale too deeply at the tempting fruity fragrance in her wake. 'I like things running to clockwork. It's the way I've always worked.'

'I never would've guessed.'

Her eyes twinkled with amusement, her lips curving into a dazzling smile that slammed into him with the force of a tumbling pyramid.

'Come on, let's go. We have business to discuss.'

'So you said on the phone.'

Her smile faded and, irrationally, he was disappointed.

'Let's wait till we reach my office so you can read the complaint for yourself.'

He found his gaze unwittingly drawn to her shoes as she fell into step beside him. The frivolous, fancy, feather shoes with barely there straps completed this outfit much better than the suit she'd worn earlier and the 'sex kitten' label instantly sprang to mind again.

Damn, he shouldn't be thinking this way, shouldn't be noticing things like sexy shoes or her alluring outfit or the way the shimmery silver on her eyelids highlighted the vivid jade depths beneath.

'You don't fit the image of the average tour guide.'

She chuckled, her soft laughter as enticing as the rest of her. 'So what does an average tour guide look like?'

'Not you,' he muttered, glad they'd reached his office. Most of the lights had been turned off at closing time and

walking along the narrow corridor hip to hip with her had him
wishing he hadn't suggested this after-hours meeting.

Proving to himself he wasn't interested in her was great
in theory. Pity the practice did little more than show him
up for fraud.

He was her boss. Which meant she was a no-go zone. Now
he just had to remember it.

Eager to get this over and done with, he flung open the door
and gestured her to enter before him.

Bad move.

If that itty-bitty skirt highlighted her incredible legs, it did
amazing things to her butt.

'Okay, let me have it.'

He wrenched his gaze up to meet hers in record time, but
the knowing smile curving her lush mouth spoke volumes:
she'd caught him checking her out and was enjoying every
minute of it.

Irritated by his slip-up, he strode to his desk and handed
her the written complaint.

'Here. Read this, then we'll discuss it.'

She sped-read it, anxiously gnawing at her bottom lip while
he tried to ignore the crazy urge to do the same.

When she reached the end, she ran a shaky hand through her
hair, inadvertently draping it over a delectably bare shoulder.

'So what do you want to do about this problem?'

Furious he couldn't keep his mind on the task at hand and
off trifling observations like the subtle glimmer of bronze
dusted on that bare shoulder, he gestured for her to have a seat
while he perched on the edge of the desk.

'This problem is indicative of a larger one, namely you.'

Her eyes flashed emerald fire while her bottom lip wobbled

ever so slightly. 'I wasn't a problem when your father hired me. He thinks I'll be an asset to the museum.'

'And do you feel the same way?'

'Of course.'

While that tremulous bottom lip suggested she was quaking inside, she locked stares with him, challenge in her green depths, taunting him to break the deadlock and look away first.

Like hell he would.

'My father may have hired you, but that doesn't mean I can't fire you.'

He dropped the magic F word and she dropped her gaze in record time.

Well, well, looked as if Miss Fancy Feet valued her job more than she let on.

'The train thing was a misunderstanding.' She handed him the complaint pro forma and sighed. 'It wasn't my fault the little monster—uh, cutie-pie—was fiddling with the display.'

How did she do that—undermine his annoyance with a hint of a smile and a blunt response?

Nothing was remotely funny about this situation—the written complaint highlighted a day filled with her incompetence—yet he had to hide his amusement before responding. 'It's an interactive display. Kids are meant to fiddle with it.'

'How was I supposed to know that?'

'It's your job to know.'

'Good point.'

Feeling like an ogre and wishing like mad she'd stop worrying that delectably full bottom lip, he said, 'You may have convinced my father to hire you for this job but I'm calling the shots now. And right now I'm less than impressed with your performance. Your résumé doesn't inspire me with confidence and neither have your skills on the first day.'

She stood so swiftly he found himself reaching out to steady her, his hands connecting with her bare arms before he had time to think.

'Look, I'm just nervous, okay? This job means a lot to me and I'm sorry for the misunderstanding with that, uh, little angel. As for the rest, I'll try to do better. Honest.'

He heard the sincerity in her voice. However, it didn't match the banked heat in her eyes and yet again he found himself contemplating the mysteries simmering beneath the surface of this vibrant woman—before mentally yelling to stay the hell away.

'Was there anything else? Because if there isn't you can probably let me go now.'

He dropped his hands in record time, unwittingly captivated by her warring vulnerability and defiance to the extent he'd forgotten he still had hold of her.

'A better effort is all I ask. So you're off to get that drink now?'

She shook her head, sending an intoxicating waft of peach and vanilla his way, instantly transporting him back twenty-five years to the rare indulgent days when his mum actually took time out to cook his favourite peach cobbler dessert.

'Bobby's not the patient type so he pretty much took off when I rang him and said I didn't know how long I'd be here.'

'Sorry,' he said, not sorry in the least.

Though he had no right to feel this way, the thought of her spending time with any guy, friend or not, looking as she did, annoyed the hell out of him.

'How sorry are you?'

'Pardon?'

'If you're really sorry, you'll make it up to me by buying me that drink I've missed out on. I've had one heck of a first day, including being dragged in here out of work hours by a very demanding boss. I'm stressed. I need to wind down.'

She tilted her chin up and tucked a curling strand of blonde silk behind her ear, befuddling his senses with her sensual scent and quirking lips.

He should've said no.

He should've cited work as a plausible excuse.

He should've remembered every sensible reason he had for pushing her away and not getting involved.

Instead, he found himself grabbing his car keys off his desk, placing a hand in the small of her back and propelling her out the door while trying not to grin as if he'd just discovered Tutankhamen's forgotten tomb.

'Lucky for you, I'm in an extremely forgiving mood. Let's go get that drink.'

CHAPTER FOUR

'IS THIS one of your regular haunts?'

Beth bit back a smile at Aidan's dubious tone. She'd been right in her assumption the stuffy boss man wouldn't frequent a place like this.

That was pretty unfair. Aidan wasn't all that stuffy considering she'd basically run a guilt trip on him earlier, not expecting he'd take her up on it. And not only had he gone for her idea he'd been laid-back, witty and charming on the way over here, regaling her with tales of his adventures overseas, making her all too aware of how downright tempting he was.

Much easier to think of him as stuffy and not her type when in fact his stories of travel, exploration and discovering hidden delights of places she'd never been to only served to add to his appeal.

As if he weren't attractive enough already!

She really needed to concentrate on doing well at this job, securing the gallery, making loads more money from selling her work and guaranteeing a stable future, something she'd craved her entire life but never had.

And doing well at this job meant not melting in a puddle at his feet every time he smiled that gorgeous, almost-dimpled smile.

Trying to delude herself into focussing on 'stuffy' and not 'sexy', she glanced around. The Loft was packed to its steel rafters with patrons draped over the expansive mirrored bar, the low, curved ruby sofas and each other, while funky acid jazz spewed out of floor-to-ceiling speakers designed to wake the dead.

'Don't worry, Professor, I'll look after you.'

She raised her cranberry martini in his direction, her hand jerking when she registered the shocked look on his face meant she'd let that little gem slip out.

'What did you just call me?'

'Professor,' she mumbled into her drink, using the glass to shield her burgeoning smile at the frown creasing his brow and making him look more professor-ish than ever.

'Why?'

She waved away his question, sloshing some of her drink onto his leg in the process.

'Oops, sorry.'

She grabbed at the napkin serving as a coaster on the table and dabbed at the spreading gin stain on his trousers.

'Leave it, it's fine,' he snapped, stilling her frantic hand while she tried not to yank hers out from under his.

If she thought he looked hot it had nothing on the effect he had on her body when he touched her.

It had taken all her will-power back in his office not to lean into him when he'd taken hold of her arms in a purely reflex gesture, the type of rescuing gesture a guy like him would make.

He was a gentleman, no two ways about it, so what was she doing here flirting with her boss?

This was madness. What had she been thinking?

She hadn't thought as usual, caught up in living for the moment, flying by the seat of her pants.

Story of her life, really.

'You didn't answer my question.' He released her hand before taking a healthy slug of his boutique beer. 'Why professor?'

'It's a term of endearment.'

She raised her martini glass in his direction before draining the rest of her drink. Better to down her drink and appear a lush than accidentally upend it over his chest.

Though if she got a chance to dab at that broad expanse of muscle because of it...

His lips twitched, drawing her attention to their shape. They looked tailor-made for imparting instructions to his employees...or for kissing crazy women not doing a very good job when their dreams depended on it.

'But we hardly know each other. Not to mention I'm your boss and have taken you to task several times today, and you find me endearing?' He shook his head, a slow smile spreading across his face. 'You're full of surprises.'

If he bowled her over with his touch, his charismatic smile slugged her with its sensual power and she cast a frantic glance towards the bar, wishing it weren't inappropriate to get tipsy in front of the boss on the first day.

'So tell me a bit about yourself—something I wouldn't know from reading your résumé.'

Twirling the delicate martini glass stem between her fingers, she decided to have a little fun. If the professor wanted her to do a better job, why not impress him with a little knowledge?

'I collect vintage hotties,' she said, trying not to giggle at his incredulous expression.

'What?'

'You know, old hot-water bottles made from porcelain.'

As if.

The only old stuff she collected came in crates, the bits of scrap metal essential for her unconventional creations.

However, Lana collected old hot-water bottles and Beth had been drilled in the finer art of what a good hottie entailed considering the museum had an extensive collection and she'd need to expound its virtues on her tours.

'Really?'

By the sardonic quirk of an eyebrow, he was having a hard time believing her. 'Tell me about them.'

Wishing she hadn't drunk her martini in record time, she tried to recall every boring detail Lana had imparted, though she doubted her cousin had envisaged the cosy couch and drinks when they'd been practising the Q and A routine.

She certainly hadn't and, while she might have a razor-sharp memory, sitting this close to him, trying to stay focussed on his eyes and not his lips, trying not to inhale for fear of copping another delicious lungful of the faintest ripe black-currant so reminiscent of her favourite Shiraz, it was increasingly difficult to string two coherent words together, let alone recall boring facts.

'Well, they date back as far as eighteen ninety. Of course, they're not practical, made from porcelain and all, but I love their uniqueness. My favourite is a cylindrical foot warmer made by Lambeth Pottery in London, closely followed by a brown ceramic hot-water bottle in the shape of a Gladstone medical bag. That one's made by Bourne Denby England. Then there's the foot warmer in the shape of a pillow, which bears the word Osokosi, a play on the phrase "oh so cosy".'

She slapped a hand over her mouth, pretending to shut herself up when in fact she couldn't remember any more of the facts she'd rote-learnt.

'Look at me, running away at the mouth. I'm sure you didn't expect such a long-winded answer.'

Something shifted in his eyes, a hint of shrewdness mingling with confusion, as if he wanted to believe her but didn't.

'On the contrary, I'm fascinated by your hobby. Tell me more.'

He was testing her. She could see it in the triumphant glitter in his eyes, in the smug smile tugging at the corners of his mouth.

Too bad she'd run out of hottie facts to bore him senseless with. Oh, hang on a second, that was her being bored out of her brain. He probably lapped up mindless drivel like this, considering he had to be fixated on old stuff to be an archae-ologist in the first place.

Faking a trill little laugh designed to distract, she placed her glass on the table in front of them and clapped her hands together.

'Uh-uh, that's enough about me. What about you? Is there more to the professor than meets the eye?'

She half expected him to tell her to knock off the profes-sor stuff, but to her surprise he slugged back the rest of his beer before answering her.

'Not much to tell. I'm an archaeologist by profession who has temporarily traded in his trowel for a briefcase.'

'Why?'

'My dad's unwell and asked me to fill in for a few months, which is about all I can handle. The thought of being stuck behind a desk for longer than that drives me crazy. I'm a nomad through and through.'

He spun the empty bottle in his hand, the expression on his face surprisingly sombre for the discussion they were having. Since when did trading small talk get so serious?

'I guess adding CEO of a museum looks good on a résumé but it doesn't compete with the thrill of the next big thing?'

'You bet.'

Though the gloss of constant travelling around as a kid had soon worn off she understood where he was coming from. She couldn't think of anything worse than being stuck in an office job, compelled to enter the same building every day, cooped up in some dingy office, seeing the same people, doing the same tasks.

Give her the freedom of working from home, when the mood struck, if her muse came out to play. Total freedom, just the way she liked it.

'What about you? Have you travelled much?'

A sad little arrow pierced her heart, embedded and lodged deep. Had she travelled? Heck, where should she start?

Around the time her mum died and her father lost the love of his life so coped by running away? How once he started moving around he couldn't stop and didn't care how it affected her? How he dragged her from town to town, school to school so she had no friends and had to put up with nicknames like geek and freak? How his endless search for something to fill the void ultimately ended in failure and left her more lost than ever?

'Mainly around Australia,' she said, quashing her memories, hating how they dragged her down. 'Travel's overrated.'

'Considering my livelihood depends on it, I'd have to disagree with you there.'

He smiled and the sadness around her heart lifted in a second, replaced by a weird breathless feeling that had her reaching for her martini glass in record time only to realise she'd finished it. 'There's nothing like the intrigue of the Forbidden City in Beijing or the architectural uniqueness of the Uspenskij Cathedral in Helsinki or the bustle of Cathedral Square in Havana.'

His eyes glowed silver in the muted light, his excitement

palpable, and she couldn't help but lean towards him, drawn by his infectious enthusiasm.

'What's your favourite city?'

'Rio de Janeiro,' he answered without a moment's hesitation, his lips curving in a delicious smile, the kind of smile that took her breath away. 'It's beautiful and filled with contrasts, from the giant Christ the Redeemer statue on Corcovado Mountain stretching its arms wide over the city to the samba parades, from the museums to the Copacabana beaches. It's a city that draws me back time and time again.'

Beth sighed, unaware she'd been holding her breath, her chin resting on her hand as he held her mesmerised. She might be a girl who craved the stability of living in one city and always had, but he sure made a great case for living out of one.

'Have I sold you? Think you'd like to visit one day?'

'Maybe.' She shrugged, her noncommittal answer drawing a curious glance.

She used to dream of travelling the world until the gloss of living out of a suitcase permanently wore off. These days, she reserved her adventurous side for creating unique designs…and exploring underlying attractions with off-limit guys—make that one guy in particular.

Eager to deflect his probing stare, she rushed on, 'So what's been your biggest discovery?'

'I'd expect an expert tour guide like yourself to know all about that.'

The teasing glint in his grey eyes held her transfixed and she sucked in a breath, his spicy scent packing as powerful a punch as the slow, sexy smile curving his lips.

She couldn't think straight when he stared at her let alone remember the question, and when he leaned forward a fraction, invading her personal space with his potent presence, and murmured, 'Well?' she did the stupidest, reckless, most impulsive thing she'd ever done.

She kissed him.

Warning bells clanged in Aidan's head as Beth closed the short distance between them and her lips touched his.

A pretty pathetic description for the mind-blowing kiss to end all kisses.

The bells intensified as she placed her hands on his chest, bracing against him while angling her mouth for better access to his.

He had a split second to react, to come to his senses and stop this insanity. For that was what it was: total and utter madness submitting to a scorching kiss from a sex kitten who happened to be an employee.

However, the moment her tongue flickered out to touch his, he threw caution to the wind and went crazy, dragging her into his arms, running his hands through the silky softness of her hair, savouring the sweetness of her mouth in a French kiss that defied description.

He lost all sense of time and place as the kiss deepened to the point where she climbed onto his lap, slid her hands up his chest to anchor behind his neck and hung on for dear life.

In fact, he would've lost it completely if not for the wolf-whistle from a nearby patron and he pulled away, a hint of cranberry on his lips and a handful of lush woman perched way too comfortably on his crotch. His very aroused crotch.

'I guess I should apologise for that,' she murmured, her gaze uncertain, her expression half dazed, half appalled as her tongue darted out to moisten her lips and he stifled a groan, desperate to pick up where they'd left off, knowing it wasn't going to happen. He wouldn't let it.

'I don't know what to say.'

He aimed for honesty rather than some lame half-assed line like, 'That was a mistake.'

Because it wasn't.

He might be a fool, he might be crazy, but he wasn't a hypocrite and after he'd spent all day insisting there wasn't a skerrick of attraction between them—and couldn't be because of their work situation—she'd blasted his reservations along with his self-delusions to kingdom come with that scintillating kiss.

Sliding off his lap and smoothing her hair as if nothing had happened, she sent him another of those part-vulnerable, part-seductress smiles.

'Then don't say anything. Let's just blame it on the atmosphere, the late hour, your tales of adventure and the tension of your new employee.'

Just like that, his passion-hazed mind cleared and clarity crashed in.

He'd just kissed his *employee*.

When he'd always maintained a strict 'no mixing business with pleasure' rule his entire career.

Hell.

He had the best analytical brain in the business and, whichever way he looked at it, what had just happened was wrong. He couldn't get involved with her no matter how much she'd blown his mind with that kiss—or how much he'd like a repeat performance, taking it all the way.

So he was attracted to her? He could handle it. As long as he didn't handle her!

He needed to get out of here, away from her intoxicating presence so he could think this through, because right now organising his thoughts was damn difficult if nigh on impossible considering the blood had drained from his brain and headed south courtesy of that incredible kiss.

'Blaming the atmosphere or the time isn't going to cut it. That kiss was way out of line.'

'You're right.' Her lips curved into a coy smile, which had him focussing on exactly how great they'd felt gliding over his. 'But it was sensational all the same.'

She leaned towards him, her warm, peachy fragrance reaching out and wrapping him in a sensual cocoon as she whispered against his ear, 'Just for the record, you kiss real well.'

Unable to stop the goofy grin spreading across his face, and knowing he had to get out of here before he did something else he'd regret—or enjoy—he held up his hands in surrender.

'I have to go. Early start tomorrow.'

'Running scared, Professor?'

Her husky voice slammed into him with the same force as the teasing glint in those striking eyes the colour of dew-dampened moss, leaving him with the same floundering feeling he'd only experienced once before when a ton of sand had caved in on a site.

Now, like then, the breath squeezed from his lungs and he had no idea whether to struggle against the odds or give in to the inevitable.

For right at that moment he knew he could struggle all he liked against the fierce attraction between them and he'd be powerless to stop it, just as he'd been unable to hold back that sand avalanche.

Ignoring her soft laughter, he shrugged into his jacket. 'Come on, I'll give you a lift home.'

'I'll take a cab, but thanks for the offer.'

Her flirtatious smile would've tempted a saint and, considering the thoughts crowding his brain at the moment were far from heavenly, he needed to get out of here. Now.

'Fine. I'll wait while you call one. Let's go.'

She laid a tentative hand on his arm and he jerked to a stop, staring at her hand as if it were a cattle prod. It had the same effect, giving him an electrical zap when he least expected it.

'This has been a bit of a crazy day for me all round and I'm sorry for overstepping the mark back there.'

She ran her other hand through her hair and he yearned to do the same, to see if the luscious gold locks felt as silky as they looked. 'I'm prone to doing impulsive things when I'm nervous.'

Leaning forwards until their noses almost touched, he murmured, 'Do I make you nervous?'

Her eyes widened, she inhaled sharply, her tongue darted out to moisten that full bottom lip he'd gladly taste again and he had his answer before she spoke.

Dropping her hand, she stepped back and he stifled a sigh of disappointment.

'This job is important to me and you're my boss so, yeah, I guess I am a little nervous.'

There she went again, surprising him with that intriguing mix of bold bluntness combined with cautious hesitancy.

He'd noticed how she'd changed the subject earlier, deftly switching the focus onto him, uncomfortable when he'd been delving into what made her tick, and he had the strangest feeling that her confidence was an act. Something—or someone—had put a susceptible chink in her sassy armour and he was curious.

What caused that vulnerable air that clung so delicately to her despite her bubbly façade? He'd give anything to find out...but he wasn't going there, remember?

'So that totally explains why I kissed you.' She gnawed on her bottom lip and clutched her bag tight. 'Nerves.'

'Uh-huh,' he said, seeing the spark of desire in her eyes and not calling her on it.

There were more than nerves at play here.

She knew it.

He knew it.

'You'll see. I'll be back to my professional best tomorrow.'

His lips twitched at the memory of her 'professional best' earlier that day.

'Tomorrow's a new day,' he said, captivated by the earnest set of her mouth, the determined gleam in her eyes, and wanting more than anything to throw his business-versus-pleasure ideals out the window at that moment and haul her back into his arms.

'Good.'

She tilted her chin up, her defiance as enchanting as the hint of timidity he glimpsed beneath. 'Trust me, you won't be disappointed. I'll be the best damn tour guide you've ever seen.'

'I look forward to it.'

Unfortunately, that wasn't the only thing he looked forward to—just the thought of seeing her rock into the museum tomorrow was enough to put a spring in his step—and with a shake of his head he propelled her out the door, determined to bundle her into a cab, head home and lose himself in a mountain of boring paperwork.

Anything to take his mind off this intriguing woman and the memory of her scintillating kiss.

CHAPTER FIVE

BETH bounced into work the next day humming under her breath.

She'd lost her mind last night when she'd kissed Aidan. But, wow, what a kiss. As far as kisses went on a scale of one to ten, it scored a massive eleven.

She'd had Aidan pegged as a highly driven, career-focussed, not-much-time-for-fun type of guy.

She'd been wrong. Wa-a-a-y wrong.

There was no way he could kiss like that if he spent all his time with his nose to the grindstone. Uh-uh. Aidan had depths to him she hadn't begun to fathom and, boy, was it going to be fun trying to explore every hidden facet.

Yeah, he was her boss and, yeah, she shouldn't go near him with a ten-foot dinosaur bone, but that kiss last night had changed everything.

She'd learned the hard way life was too short not to make the most of every opportunity and right now Aidan Voss looked like one big, delicious opportunity wrapped up in a designer suit.

'Hi, Beth.'

She stopped at the tentative tap on her shoulder and swivelled to face Dorothy.

'Morning. How are you?'

'Great.'

Dorothy tugged self-consciously at her burgundy fitted jacket flaring at the hips and sitting rather well over a matching pencil skirt. 'Thanks for helping me choose this outfit yesterday. I feel like a new woman.'

'You're welcome.'

Beth smiled, trying to focus on the suit and avert her gaze from Dorothy's staid navy pumps, whose scuff marks were poorly hidden by a shade of blue almost as hideous as the shoes themselves. 'How about we do a bit of shoe shopping today at lunchtime?'

The young woman's face fell. 'I can't. I'm filling in for one of the temps in the Science and Life Gallery.'

'No worries, we'll do it tomorrow.'

Dorothy's ecstatic expression turned the girl from mousy to beautiful in a second and Beth smiled, telling herself that it was her duty to share her shoe expertise with her fellow women.

She glanced at her watch and grimaced. 'Sorry, Dot. Love to stay and chat but the boss man might be on the warpath.'

Dorothy snapped her fingers. 'I forgot. Mr Voss wants to see you.'

'Oh-oh, what have I done now?' she muttered under her breath, before thanking Dorothy and heading up to his office.

The kitten heels of her new designer butterscotch court shoes clattered along the marble corridor and she wriggled her toes, preferring open-toe sandals any day.

Funny, as she planned on slipping into a pair any moment now...

She really shouldn't do this considering she'd been trying to convince Aidan of her professionalism at the end of last night, but she'd seen the spark in his eyes, the devilish glint that told her their attraction was entirely mutual.

Besides, there was no harm in having a little laugh on the job. It fostered good workplace relations…it was team-building…great for employee morale and all that guff.

Smiling, she pulled up outside Aidan's door and cast a quick glance up and down the corridor, reassured it was empty, before slipping a pair of fabulous mulberry spangly sandals out of her bag, kicking off the court shoes and reacquainting her feet with a familiar pair of old friends.

'That's better.' Her grin turned positively smug as she admired the contrast of her Knockout Cherry toenails against the deep purple satin strap covering her forefoot. 'Much better.'

Schooling her face into serious mode was hard work considering the persistent smile threatening to break through as she envisaged Aidan's expression when he laid eyes on her shoes, but she managed it in time to knock sharply at his door and enter after his muffled, 'Come in.'

'You wanted to see me?'

She knew the exact moment he noticed the shoes for he stopped dead in his tracks halfway across the office, his slate gaze riveted to her feet.

'What the hell are those?'

He pointed to her Jimmy Choos and she wriggled her toes in response.

'Would you believe I had another shoe crisis on the way in today?'

His gaze snapped up to meet hers, stormy grey warring with cheeky green.

'No.'

'Would you believe the dog ate my work shoes?'

'No.'

'How about I got held up by the shoe police for wearing low heels and to avoid being arrested I had to wear these?'

'You're pushing your luck.'

The corners of his mouth twitched, in total contrast to the frown marring his brow. 'I told you to wear appropriate footwear today.'

Unable to contain her laughter a second longer, she chuckled and slid the court shoes out of her bag.

'Relax, Professor, I was just teasing you.'

His lips stilled and his expression darkened. 'Like last night?'

Surprised he'd brought up the kiss, she perched on the edge of an overstuffed chair and swapped shoes. 'Don't sweat it. I hope you didn't lose any sleep over what happened. I certainly didn't.'

Checking out her shoes and wrinkling her nose at the come-down in height, she thrust the purple Choos into her bag and looked up at him from beneath her mascara-ed lashes.

'As sensational as it was and all, it's not worth worrying about. So, what did you want to see me about?'

Gotcha! She watched male pride war with indignation, knowing he'd be torn between discussing her flattery further and wanting to forget the kiss ever happened. Sadly, it looked as if his common sense kicked in as he walked around his desk and took a seat in an imposing leather chair that looked as uncomfortable as the one she sat on.

'There's been a change of plans.'

He picked up a piece of expensive ivory paper that looked suspiciously like her résumé and rattled it in her direction.

'I know you were going to spend the first few weeks conducting tours in the Australia Gallery and helping out with organising a few workshops to familiarise yourself with the museum, but I need you to do more.'

The bubble of happiness that sustained her through most days popped as the implication of his words sank in. It had been hard work swotting up on all the info required to take tours of one gallery; imagine how much time she'd have to invest for more. And what with organising paperwork for the lease and completing her latest sculpture…help!

He continued, oblivious to her escalating tension. 'I think the quickest way to get you up to speed is throw you in the deep end and, what with the flu bug hitting us hard at the moment and staff going down almost daily, I want you to take on the Bunjilaka Aboriginal Centre and the Mind and Body Gallery too.'

Great. She might need this job to secure her own gallery, but what would be the point if she didn't have any pieces to fill it? She needed time to sculpt, but with swotting up on these new areas of the museum at night she wouldn't have a free moment.

She'd have to tell him.

But what about her 'you can trust me, I'll be the best damn tour guide you've ever seen' spiel she'd given him last night? If she backed down now and said she couldn't do it would he chalk it up as another mark against her or, worse, fire her?

Clutching her bag to her chest, somewhat comforted by the stab of stiletto through the soft leather, she racked her brain for a quick-fire response. However, before she could come up with anything suitable he handed her a bulging manila folder.

'Here. I know it's a lot to take in but I need you up to scratch asap. You'll find information on those two galleries in here.'

'When would you like me to start taking tours in the new galleries?'

'Tomorrow.'

His direct stare unnerved her more than his unreasonable timeframe. For a fairly straightforward 'what you see is what you get' type of guy, his eyes glittered with triumph, as if he knew she wasn't up to her professional promise and had called her on it.

Floundering for something characteristically witty to say and coming up lacking, she gripped her bag tighter and opted for partial honesty.

'I appreciate your faith in me, but I'm feeling a little over-whelmed, what with getting used to the one gallery, acquainting myself with the layout and staff—'

'Either you can do it or you can't.' He cut her off, his tone razor-sharp and brooking no argument. 'And if you can't… well, I guess we'd have to re-evaluate your contract.'

Damn and blast the man! The laid-back, sexy guy from last night had morphed back into the powerful CEO and she didn't like the change one bit.

As for re-evaluating…no way she'd let that happen. Losing this job wasn't an option.

'Of course I can do it.'

Squaring her shoulders, she released her death grip on her bag, knowing she'd have to do some quick thinking to come up with a workable solution to this doozy of a problem. She might have a photographic memory, but cramming in a folder's worth of tour-guide expertise in one night would be impossible.

Aidan would know it.

With a mental 'duh', it hit her. This was a test.

Maybe he really did want to get rid of her and was expecting her to fail spectacularly so he'd have no other option but to fire her?

Well, she had news for him.

She'd faced worse growing up, having to think on her feet to avoid taunts and bullies at every new school, using her brain to outwit and outsmart, learning to distance herself from criticism from teachers and kids who had no idea about her home life.

She'd practised putting on a brave face while she'd hurt on

the inside, learned to shield her real emotions behind a confident front and a smart mouth.

But she couldn't push her luck here. If this was some warped test she had no intention of failing. If it wasn't, maybe she could buy some time?

With a poised smile far removed from the jumble of nerves tumbling in her belly, she grabbed the manila folder and stuffed it into her bag.

'I totally understand how tough it is around here at the moment with less staff, but how about you give me a few more days to look over this and I'll start the new tours next week?'

The tiny crease between his brows had reappeared, doing little to distract from his handsome face. 'How many days do you need?'

'How about the rest of the week? That way, I can swot over the weekend too and be up to scratch to wow the masses first thing Monday.'

Sending him her best dazzling smile, she waited for a reaction.

He made her sweat for it, studying her face as if searching for one of his precious old artefacts before allowing his lips to curve into a beguiling smile, the type of smile that could charm the pants off a girl.

If she were prone to that sort of thing.

'Fine, have it your way.'

'Great.' She leaped out of the chair, eager to make her escape while the going was good.

'For now,' he added, reasserting his power with the finesse of a businessman used to mixing subtlety with an iron-clad will.

'Thanks, I'm sure you'll be impressed.'

She hefted her bag with the ten-ton-tome of information under her arm and sent him a casual wave as she headed for the door, relieved that he'd given her a reprieve. With a little bit of luck—and a lot of hard work—she could juggle her two jobs without letting any balls slip.

'I already am.'

She turned at the door, the husky timbre of his voice alerting her to the fact that maybe, hopefully, he wasn't only referring to her work skills.

Sure enough, his gaze slid from her legs upwards and she sent him a coy smile, buoyed by the gleam of male apprecia- tion in those incredibly expressive silver eyes.

They might have dismissed that kiss last night as an aber- ration, but there was no denying the sizzle of attraction buzzing between them, professionalism or not.

'I can always slip the other shoes back on if you like?'

'For a woman perilously close to having me revoke those few extra days' grace I've just given you, you're mighty sure of yourself,' he said, grudging admiration in the hint of a smile.

'I know what I want and I know how to get it.'

She paused, letting her gaze drift to his lips before rising ever so slowly to reconnect with his smoky eyes again. 'After last night, you of all people should know that.'

Humming Prince's 'Kiss' under her breath, she walked out the door.

'Damn and blast it!'

Dorothy sent her a scandalous glance as if she'd just dropped the F bomb. 'Don't worry, we're only a few minutes late.'

Beth practically ran the last few metres to the museum entrance, uncharacteristically grateful she wasn't wearing her stilettos for once. 'I know, but I've got a teenage school-group tour I have to lead.'

And the boss is tagging along to see how I'm doing.

That thought alone lent her extra speed and she flew through the door and waved to Dorothy over her shoulder. 'Later, Dot.'

'Thanks for taking me shoe shopping,' Dorothy called out, her wistful tone bringing Beth up short.

The young woman was a walking fashion disaster and she couldn't leave her hanging, not when she'd promised her a makeover to go with her new outfits and shoes.

'I'll see you tomorrow and we'll tee up a time then for your makeover, okay?'

'Great.'

Dorothy's beaming smile could've lit a path for the space shuttle to follow. 'I really appreciate what you're doing for me, Beth. You're the best.'

Ha! If only Aidan thought so too.

Waving, Beth dashed into the Mind and Body Gallery, tugging down her blazer with one hand while tucking a stray strand of hair back into the loose French twist at the nape of her neck with the other.

She didn't know what was more annoying, the way the chartreuse jacket edged in ecru kept riding up over her hips or the headache that came with wearing her hair confined in a knot for a touch of added professionalism today. With Aidan watching her every move during her first tour in this new gallery, she had to look the part even if she felt like the least qualified person on the planet to conduct it.

Please let him be late, she thought, her gaze darting around the room while she simultaneously managed a confident smile at the biology students waiting for her.

While the kids crowded around her, thrusting their hands in the air and firing questions before she'd even started, her gaze collided with a cool grey one at the back of the group, disapproval clear in its depths.

Great. Looked like the punctuality professor had already chalked up another black mark next to her name.

Determined to ignore him, she focussed all her attention on the kids, who proceeded to make the next hour the most tedious, harassed, nightmarish sixty minutes of her entire life.

They hassled her.

They laughed at her.

One of the guys had the audacity to lay a hand on her butt as he pretended to jostle for a front position in the group.

If Aidan hadn't been around she might've been tempted to do something very unprofessional—such as replace the human brain model with the real thing from that hormonal little creep—but as it was she grinned, she extolled the virtues of the human body and answered questions as best she could.

Which obviously wasn't good enough considering Aidan summoned her to his office when the tour ended. He didn't even have the decency to give her time for a recovery coffee.

'I'll see you in ten minutes,' he said, tapping his watch as if she didn't know what it was or couldn't tell the time—okay, so he had a point there considering she'd been late several times—frown in place, not a glimmer of a smile.

She nodded, too tired to respond, too despondent to fire back a witty quip.

This was it. Her best wasn't good enough.

And as she trudged the long corridor like a recalcitrant kid summoned to the principal's office, she couldn't think of one damn thing to do about it.

Pulling up outside Aidan's door, she knocked sharply, all business and no play, the exact opposite of her visit to his inner sanctum last week.

However, while she trembled inside, she wouldn't let it show. Brave front at all costs. It was a motto she lived by, a motto tried and tested many times with her dad as he'd shut the door on her needs time and time again.

Now, like then, she wouldn't let her nerves get the better of her, wouldn't let it rattle her.

Brave front, brave front, she mentally recited and at Aidan's barked, 'Come in,' she took a deep breath, entered the room and stalked to his desk, shoulders squared and on the defensive.

'What did you think of the tour?'

Admiration shot through Aidan as he stared at the pink-cheeked, unusually subdued woman standing before him.

She should be quaking in her boots right now, but, apart from the faint blush staining her cheeks and the rigid posture, Beth showed little sign of being flustered.

He had a feeling what he was about to say would change all that.

'Take a seat.'

He waved towards the chair opposite, not surprised she sat quickly. For once he had Miss Fancy Feet on the back foot, no pun intended, and, rather than feeling good about it, he hated that she saw him as some bossy ogre.

Though maybe it was a good thing having her stare at him with wariness rather than her usual sassy sparkle. It was hard enough having her work here every day, bouncing around the place with a sunny smile on her face, without dragging her into this office with work the furthest thing from his mind. At least this way he got to play the big, bad boss and she'd maintain a circumspect distance. He hoped.

'Let's discuss your skills as a tour guide, shall we?'

Just mentioning the tour had him thinking icebergs and blizzards and anything frigid, for it had taken all his will-power not to haul her out of that tour and into the nearest janitor's closet to have his wicked way with her. She'd been bold and sweet and oh-so-sexy and he couldn't stand this tension much longer.

She didn't blink or flinch or fiddle and his admiration went up another notch.

'I wasn't that bad.'

'Actually, you're right. I could tell you'd studied the information I gave you last week but, unfortunately, it isn't enough.'

He watched, transfixed, as she worried her bottom lip and he folded his arms, tucking them in nice and tight to avoid reaching out, tumbling her onto his lap, cuddling her close and wiping away the glimmer of fear in her eyes.

'You're not a very tolerant man.'

Her bravado was staggering. Even when faced with a performance review she continued to dish it out to him. And rather than getting riled, he fought the impulse to applaud.

'On the contrary, I'm very tolerant. I've worked with people of different work ethics all around the world. I've worked through strikes, floods, even the odd plague of unwanted insects. But I must say I've never worked with anyone quite like you before.'

'It takes all types to make the world go round.'

'Correction, it takes all working types and that's one thing you're not quite up to scratch with, and that's work.'

Though that wasn't entirely true. Beth might not know how to work as a tour guide to the standards he expected, but she sure knew how to work it. With every step she took, with every sensual swivel of her hips, with every toss of her head and with every seductive smile, she knew how to work every gorgeous inch to her advantage.

Take today, for instance. Who else had the confidence to stroll in late for a tour group, pretend he weren't there and then handle a bunch of hyperactive teenagers without losing control?

He'd been captivated from the second she'd locked gazes with him and proceeded to act as if he didn't exist, and, while he'd been impressed by how much knowledge she'd crammed over the last week, it had been her natural exuberance that had more than made up for any shortfall in skills.

She attempted a haughty glare, but it didn't work, considering her eyes shimmered with disappointment, and he fisted his hands to stop from reaching out to her.

The über-confident, sassy Fancy Feet he could handle; her subdued, chastened counterpart almost undid him completely.

'I can assure you I know what hard work is and, if you'd just give me a chance, I can prove it to you. I just need more time to get up to speed—'

'That's why I called you in here.'

He hated the slight shoulder slump, the dejection lingering around her down-turned mouth, the same mouth that felt so incredible moving with innate sensuality beneath his own.

After the way he'd been coming down on her, she probably thought he was going to fire her and it didn't sit well with him. He was usually a fair boss, willing to cut his workers a little slack, but for some reason he'd been harder on Beth than most.

Some reason? Try the fact he couldn't get her out of his head and the accompanying guilt of seeing an employee that way was the main reason for his strident, inflexible tyranny.

But not any more. He could see how hard she was trying and it wasn't her fault he couldn't keep his thoughts strictly professional.

'Look, Beth, I can see you've tried and I admire that. But doing this job requires more than swotting up on a bunch of facts and flashing a charming smile. I want someone with a genuine love for this place, for the displays, someone who can impart that enthusiasm during their tours. You're bright and bubbly and have put in a huge effort, but I want you to take this to the next level. And I'm willing to help you do it.'

She gnawed at her bottom lip, unwittingly drawing his attention to its plumpness, its softness and the way it moulded so perfectly to his when she kissed.

'You want to *help* me?'

Her incredulous expression confirmed his suspicion that she'd expected him to fire her, making him feel lower than the deepest earth-bound fossil.

'That's right.' He nodded and pushed a list across the desk towards her. 'Here's a list of the displays in each gallery. Reading a whole heap of facts from the manuals I gave you can be pretty dry, so why don't I give you a feel for them first-hand? I love all the stuff in this place and it makes sense to get you up to scratch quickly so you'll have an added authority when taking the tours.'

Shaking her head, she fixed him with a bemused stare. 'Thanks for the offer, it sounds great, but, I have to tell you, I'm surprised.'

No more than him. If he'd been smart, he would've given her her marching orders, taking her out of arm's reach before he took this attraction a step further than that unforgettable kiss.

But he couldn't do it to her. He'd never met anyone so enthused, so hell-bent on succeeding with something they knew little about, and he admired her for it.

He'd always been a reasonable boss on the digs he'd supervised and, while being stuck behind this desk mightn't be a career highlight for him, the time he was here he intended to make good. A good CEO would foster Beth's professional development, not sever it because he couldn't get a handle on his swinging libido.

'You thought I was going to give you a hard time?'

'Uh-huh.'

'I'm not that bad, am I?'

Her eyes lost their wary glint, replaced by her signature daring. 'Fishing for compliments, Professor?'

'I don't need to fish.'

'I guess you don't, considering the bait.'

Oh, she was good. With her beguiling green eyes a sensual flinty jade as they slid over him and an enticing curve to her lips, she was a woman on a mission: to drive him slowly but surely crazy.

He needed to focus on business, keep his mind on the job. It was the only way to cope with his insane, driving need to possess this woman, every delicious inch of her.

'Getting back to the displays, I'll tee up a few after-hour sessions and we'll get started asap, okay?'

Her lips curved into a smug smile as if she knew exactly how he'd like to get started—with her.

'Thanks, you won't regret it.'

As she sashayed out the door and he couldn't tear his gaze off her long legs he knew it was too late. He already did.

CHAPTER SIX

'I'VE READ a bit about this one. Could you tell me more about the history behind the Glozel Runes?'

Beth exhaled, a long low breath that whooshed out of her lungs and sounded like a childish huff in the silence as she waited for her first history lesson of the evening.

She should be home sculpting the latest shipment of metal delivered that morning, but instead here she was, alone, with her sexy boss—not that she should be noticing that sort of thing—swotting up on boring artefacts to keep her job.

Crooking his finger at her, he leaned forward and laid his palm against the glass cabinet, the excitement in his face showing her how much he'd like to touch the ancient stones for real.

'In nineteen twenty-four, a farmer ploughing in Glozel, near Vichy in France, discovered an underground chamber. His grandson pulled out a clay tablet covered in characters they couldn't decipher so they found a local amateur archaeologist who said the tablets dated back to eight thousand BC. However, some experts now think the runes are forgeries so there's always been a bit of a battle over them. There have been similar rune finds in China and even here in Australia but the writing can't be deciphered.'

She leaned forward till her nose almost pressed against the

glass cabinet, squinting and tilting her head. 'Looks like a bunch of squiggles to me. Though some of the shapes look vaguely like the alphabet?'

He sent her a speculative glance. 'You're right, but deciphering what they mean is still considered to be almost impossible by the experts. Some say Celtic pilgrims inscribed some of these pieces later, around seven hundred to one thousand BC, but no one knows for sure.'

'Interesting.'

When Lana had been expounding the virtues of various museum displays Beth had been bored out of her brain and her eyes had glazed over. However, something shifted as Aidan's encouraging smile lit her from within, his animated expression turning his face from ruggedly handsome to drop-dead gorgeous.

Nothing like a man with passion for his job, and if he was this passionate about work, imagine what he'd be like at play...

'Okay, I think I've got a handle on the runes. How about we move on to the Ica Stones next?'

She needed to refocus on work, had to concentrate her attention on the display in front of her rather than the ardent gleam in his eyes.

He clearly loved what he did and as he beckoned her closer to look at the strange, misshapen hunks of stone she couldn't help but absorb some of his excitement.

'This group of stones was found near the Peruvian city of Ica in nineteen sixty-one. An analysis of the geological sedimentation indicated the images were over ten thousand years old but the date was contradicted by the objects and living creatures depicted in the images because they couldn't possibly have existed at that time.'

'What were the pictures?'

'Check it out.'

She had no option but to almost snuggle into him, peering through the glass where he pointed, trying not to inhale his delicious spicy blackcurrant scent and blow her concentration sky-high.

'See over there? That image looks like a person using a telescope to observe the heavens. And that one over there looks like tools performing heart surgery on an anatomically correct heart.'

'Weird.'

But there was nothing weird about her visceral reaction to the sexy archaeologist with fervour in his voice and passion in his eyes.

He made the artefacts come alive and for a brief, irrational moment she could see herself exploring alongside him, absorbing his energy, fascinated by his finds.

'You're enjoying this more than you expected?'

Her rueful grin spoke volumes. 'I am. You're a good teacher, Professor.'

'I love what I do.'

'It shows.'

Beth didn't know how long they stayed there, shoulder to shoulder, staring into each other's eyes, but the electricity between them was palpable, the air fairly crackling with it, and she found herself gravitating towards him, wishing he'd kiss her, hold her, do a million and one wild things with her.

'Let's move on.'

He sprung up, unfolding his long frame from its squatting position to perch on a nearby chair in typical alpha male pose, towering over her in an attempt to regain the upper hand after she'd rattled him.

'If you've had enough in this gallery, we can move on to the next.'

She had two options: pretend the unbelievable sexual tension between them didn't exist or push him to acknowledge it and do something about it.

The first would be the safe, sensible option. Since when had she done sensible?

'Ignoring this won't make it go away.'

His gaze snapped to hers, the smoky grey depths unreadable, but he didn't speak, just folded his arms, maintaining his distance, trying to appear the cool, unflappable boss. He would've pulled it off too if it weren't for that scar under his right eyebrow that moved imperceptibly, the same small movement she'd noticed right before she'd kissed him at the bar on her first day.

She affected him no matter how much he wanted to ignore her or pretend the spark between them didn't exist.

But she'd never been any good at pretending; just ask her dad, who'd known her enthusiasm for every new place they'd settled was fake no matter how hard she'd tried to disguise it. She'd eventually given up the act and had pleaded with him countless times to stay in one place long enough to build a life for them, but it hadn't changed a thing.

'I'm not ignoring anything,' he said, his offhand tone at total odds with the banked heat simmering in those mysterious grey depths.

'You know what I'm talking about.'

She took a step towards him, enjoying the slight flicker of alarm flash across his face, as if he expected her to launch herself at him and ravage him on the spot.

He wished. Actually, no, that was her.

Frowning, he swiped a hand over his face. 'I can't discuss this with you. You just have to leave it alone.'

Reaching out, she laid a hand on his arm and he jumped

as if she'd electrocuted him, and as his gaze riveted to hers she knew *this* definitely needed confronting.

'It doesn't have to be this way, you know,' she murmured, trapped beneath the burning intensity of his stare, her breath catching at the smouldering desire in his eyes.

'Yes, it does.'

His yearning expression made a mockery of his words and he didn't flinch or shrug off her hand or move a millimetre when she slid her palm over the expensive cool wool of his designer jacket slowly upwards until it rested on his bicep, the muscle flexing deliciously beneath her tingling palm.

'I know this has the potential to be awkward, but it doesn't have to be.'

She hoped her touch conveyed that she understood, that he wasn't the only one caught up in this spellbinding attraction, that they could handle it even if working together.

'Awkward? That's an understatement.'

With a shake of his head, he stepped away, turning his back on her to lean against the back of the chair, arms outstretched, leaving her with a tempting view of his butt.

Oh, yeah, there was definitely some major attraction going on here and it wasn't all one-sided.

But what could she do if he didn't acknowledge it? They couldn't go on pretending it didn't exist, if even the most innocuous of time spent together such as him showing her the ropes around here ended up with them in an almost clinch.

Injecting lightness into her tone, she said, 'Look, why don't we get out of here?'

'Why?'

He swivelled to face her, his expression comical, as if she'd just asked him to strip down and get naked with her in front of his precious Ica Stones.

'My head's spinning with facts. I think it would do us both good to get away from here for a while, clear the air a bit, so why don't we go grab a coffee and have a chat?'

His jaw clenched, the tiny muscle near the scar on his right eyebrow twitched, but his molten silver eyes still hadn't lost their 'I want you but I'm trying to fight it' expression.

'I don't want to do this.'

'I know you don't, but it won't be too heavy, promise. Just a little friendly conversation over the best cake you've ever eaten, accompanied by coffee to die for.'

'You can't be referring to the cafeteria.'

His wry smile showed her she did have a shot at this, just as she suspected. For all his CEO bluster Aidan was a bit of a softie beneath that tough, sexy exterior. And if she could just get him to face up to this thing between them…

'Actually, I was thinking more along the lines of Brunetti's.'

'Never been there.'

She pretended a mock swoon with a dramatic hand to the forehead. 'You haven't lived in Melbourne very much, have you?'

He shook his head.

'Brunetti's is an institution. Come on, you absolutely, positively have to try it. You'll thank me.'

She stood and smoothed her jacket, her eagerness to get to the fabulous café having as much to do with getting Aidan to a guaranteed packed public place before she launched herself at him as consuming the mouth-watering delicacies the place was famous for.

'You're the most exasperating woman I've ever met.' He pushed off the chair with a resigned sigh, sending her a 'this better be good' glare.

'In that case, you need a great piece of cake. Quality cake is balm to a weary soul like yours.'

'You're crazy.'

He shook his head while shrugging into his jacket.

And you love me for it.

Thankfully, she thought before she spoke for once and, sending him her best bewitching smile, she preceded him out of the gallery.

'Okay, I'll admit it. You were right.'

'Told you. Always trust a woman when it comes to good cake.'

Beth grinned before taking a bite out of a gigantic chocolate confection, the flaky pastry melting on her tongue alongside the creamy custard filling. 'So, is your soul soothed yet?'

Waving his fork at her, Aidan sent her a glare with all the force of a giant pussycat. 'Not while you keep staring at me the same way you're looking at that chocolate thing you're gobbling.'

'Oh, and how's that?'

'You know damn well. Now, let me finish this cake in peace,' he muttered, his expression wary as he forked the last piece of white chocolate mud cake from his plate into his mouth.

Enjoying herself way too much, she leaned forward a fraction, delighting at the tortured expression that flicked across his face as he glanced at her cleavage and away in less than a second.

'Good idea, eat up. I have a feeling what we're about to discuss may give you indigestion.'

'You've already done that.'

He tried a mock frown and failed, and she laughed; nobody could stay mad for long while savouring a Brunetti's delight.

Maybe she should order him the entire mouth-watering display in the front counter considering what she was about to do.

Laying down his fork and pushing his empty cappuccino cup away, he folded his arms.

'I suppose now is as good a time as any to talk about this.'

Stuffing the last of the mignon into her mouth to buy time, she held up a finger to ask for a minute. Now they were here and it was crunch time to face this attraction simmering between them, suddenly her confidence had gone AWOL.

Confronting it was one thing, talking about it with those intense grey eyes locked on hers another.

Well, here goes nothing.

Savouring the last silky slide of chocolate custard down her throat, she washed it down with a sip of latte before leaning back in her chair and sending him a beguiling smile.

'First up, I want you to promise you'll hear me out.'

A fine line appeared between his brows as he leaned forward, his face mere inches from hers.

'Just cut to the chase.'

She didn't move, momentarily captivated by the warmth of his breath fanning against her cheek and the hint of coffee on his breath, knowing if she broached the short distance between them and laid her lips on his, he'd taste like the sweetest decadent chocolate blended with superb coffee.

'Beth…' His warning growl roused her and she blinked, pulling away before she followed through on yet another insane impulse to kiss him.

Taking a great gulp of air, her lungs flooding with his spicy blackcurrant scent mingled with aromatic coffee, she knew it was now or never. She had nothing to lose.

'I'm attracted to you,' she blurted, clasping her hands in her lap to stop from reaching out, grabbing his lapels and shaking that impassive mask off his face. 'And I'm guessing the feeling's mutual but you're reluctant to get involved because we work together. I'm also guessing we'd have a lot of fun together given half a chance.'

He sat bolt upright, as if she'd prodded him with her fork, and she quickly continued before she lost her nerve. 'You're an adventurous guy and adventurous guys take risks. They take chances on things even though on face value they probably shouldn't. And that's what I'm asking you to do. Take a chance on me.'

On us, was what she was really saying, and by the astute gleam in his eyes he knew it too.

'You don't mince words, do you?'

She shrugged, thankful he was honest enough not to deny it. 'What's the point? I've always been up front. I say it how it is.'

Shaking his head, he ran a hand over his face before fixing her with that steady grey-eyed gaze that did delicious, tummy-tumbling things to her insides.

'I could give you the brush-off but that wouldn't be fair, considering you're right.'

If her tummy had tumbled with a single look from him, it leaped and punched the air at his admission.

'So you're attracted to me?'

His rueful smile spoke volumes. 'I think it was that kiss that did it.'

'And don't forget the shoes.' She leaned forward and whispered behind her hand, 'You seem to have a thing for those.'

His spontaneous laughter warmed her better than the fabulous lattes she always ordered here.

'So now that all this attraction business is out in the open, what are we going to do about it?'

His laughter petered out as he rubbed the back of his neck

as if she'd given him an ache there. Yep, that was her, a real pain in the neck when she wanted something, just as her dad had always said.

With him, all she'd ever wanted was a little attention, some sign he loved her enough to put her needs first rather than his stupid quest to obliterate her mum's memory by traipsing around the countryside in the search of goodness knew what. Pity what she'd wanted she rarely got back then. Hopefully things would be different with Aidan now.

'Do about this crazy attraction? Don't ask.'

She batted her eyelashes at him, sending him a coy smile designed to tease. 'And what's so crazy about it? I'm pretty cute, you know.'

He smiled, a genuine, easygoing smile that transformed his face to off-the-scale gorgeous in a second.

'Yeah, I know. That's half the problem. I can't seem to forget it.'

'And what's the other half?'

His eyes darkened to stormy pewter as he leaned forward and murmured, 'How much I want you.'

'Oh…' she breathed out on a sigh, desperate to close the short distance and kiss him, to leap across the table and straddle his lap, to wrap her arms around him till he had no choice but to admit how fantastic it would be to give in to the heat searing between them.

'But we can't always have what we want.'

He broke the spell by leaning back and folding his arms as if trying to ward her off. As if that would work.

Matching his serious tone, she wriggled back in her chair and laid her hands palm-up in front of him. 'Look, no tricks up these sleeves.

'You know what I want?' Apart from you. 'I want to give

this job all I've got. I want to be a success at it and you helping me means a lot. I promise I won't let anything at work interfere with…us.'

His right eyebrow twitched, the scar beneath it doing a little dance at the mention of 'us', but apart from that one tell-tale sign, no reaction. Not a glimmer of a smile. No amused glint in those slate eyes.

Nothing.

In desperation, she grabbed a serviette off the table and twisted it in her lap, gnawing at her bottom lip before she said something she'd regret, like, Take me, I'm yours.

When ten seconds stretched to thirty and the napkin lay shredded in her lap along with her fading hope, some of her old fire kicked in.

'Well? Are you going to keep me in suspense for ever or do you want me to beg?'

She bit the tip of her tongue as his eyes finally sparked, the shooting heat sizzling her all the way down to her toes. Heck, even if he said no, what hope did she have of maintaining her distance? She had as much chance of following through on that as resisting anything chocolaty in the window any time she walked past this place.

Steepling his fingers together, he leaned forward, rested his elbows on the table and smiled, an utterly spellbinding, irresistible smile that left her quivering with desire.

'Begging might be fun.'

Realisation dawned in that moment. He was going to give them a chance.

'Fabulous!'

Before she could think twice she jumped up from her seat, leaned across the table, grabbed hold of his head and planted an impulsive kiss on his lips.

She'd meant it as a brief, spur-of-the-moment, I-can't-believe-this-is-happening kiss.

However, it soon turned into something more as she registered the soft warmth of his mouth beneath hers, the feel of the faintest stubble against her palms and the stimulating taste of coffee and wickedly delicious chocolate lingering on his lips.

Wishing she could stay like this for ever, savouring the sensations assailing her body, she reluctantly sat back down with a defiant toss of her hair, bracing for a warning that aberrant kisses in public shouldn't happen.

His warm smile took her completely by surprise.

'If that's what I get for a bit of mild flirting, I'd sure like to see what's in store when I actually try and charm you.'

Her heart kicked over at the power packed behind that smile and the implication behind his words while she wondered for the umpteenth time what it was about this guy that had her so hot and bothered.

He wore designer suits and sedate ties; she preferred jeans and T-shirts on her guys.

His hair was short and too tidy; she preferred long around the collar and unruly.

He was a CEO, she preferred creative guys, musos and artists and writers, guys who didn't conform.

Then why couldn't she stop thinking about him, let alone control her hormones? She heated from the inside out whenever he looked at her and as for their sparring…if he only knew how much a quick comeback and quicker wit turned her on.

Then again, maybe she was protesting too much? Maybe his latent adventurous side matched hers all too well? Maybe it scared the living daylights out of her how quickly she'd acted on their attraction? How much she'd like to take it further given half a chance?

More flustered than she cared to admit, she wriggled in her chair. 'So, you think you can charm me, huh?'

Aidan watched Beth squirm, her hands shifting from fidgeting with the sugar sachets on the table to tucking stray strands of hair into her bun to toying with the cutlery.

And he inwardly smiled. He'd never met anyone so impulsive, so spontaneous, so downright amazing.

Even now he couldn't believe she'd been gutsy enough to confront him like this and verbalise their attraction, and silently applauded her bravado.

'Well?'

Her smooth brow puckered and he wondered if her skin felt as velvety-soft as it looked. He'd fantasised about how she'd feel ever since that kiss the other night, though in his dreams he didn't just stop at feeling.

He imagined how she'd whisper his name as he caressed every inch of her body, how she'd moan as he tasted her, how she'd plead for more as she arched against him as he entered her...

'If you're going to make me wait for your answer, I guess it's not so bad if you look at me like that.'

Snapping back to attention, he stared at her, the faint pink of her cheeks and the knowing smile playing about her lips telling him she knew exactly what kind of effect she had on him.

Damn it, he shouldn't even be contemplating this.

Searching for artefacts around the world usually gave him a buzz, but without his precious job he needed something in his life, a touch of exuberance, of excitement, something to make his blood fizz. The kind of thing that Beth had going on...in spades.

When she entered a room, everything seemed brighter.

When she opened her mouth and dropped one of her typical gems, everything seemed funnier.

And considering stepping into the CEO job for his father even for a limited time wasn't quite as satisfying as he'd imagined, he needed a spark in his life and that spark was Beth Walker.

Knowing what he was about to do was absolute madness but desperate to get some of his old enthusiasm back, he said, 'Oh, yeah, I *know* I can charm you.'

One of her eyebrows formed a perfectly inverted V, challenging him, teasing him. 'You do know that I won't be immune to your charms? And that we'll probably take this all the way?'

'I know.'

There was no denying the chemistry between them any longer and, while he'd been a stickler in the past for not mixing business with pleasure, he now had no choice. He had to make an exception to the general rule, for his gut instincts screamed Beth Walker was worth it.

'This is going to be fun.'

She clapped her hands and beamed, her dazzling smile hitting him like a punch to the gut, leaving him gasping for air. When she smiled at him like that, it wasn't only sparks that shot through him, but a cartload of fireworks, the whole damn exploding shebang.

'You're the best, Professor.'

With her lips curved in a delicious smile, a cheeky glint in her sparkling eyes and the lingering scent of peaches and vanilla clinging to his lapel where she'd grabbed him, he knew he was in way over his head.

'Now we've established there's something going on here that both of us have absolutely no control over, can we get back to work?'

Glancing at her watch, she screwed up her pert nose. 'I'm

beat. Do you mind if I head home and we pick up on the history lessons tomorrow evening?'

'Sure, though I need to run something by you before tomorrow. I have a job for you.'

'Name it.' She snapped her fingers, all bright-eyed enthusiasm.

'Actually, it's not too arduous and doesn't involve hoicking around any encyclopaedias of knowledge.'

'Sounds like a piece of cake.'

Her gaze drifted longingly towards the front counter brimming with baked goods and he briefly wondered if she was as zealous about anything else as she was for sweet things.

Damn, he had it bad. He'd known this would happen. As soon as he'd acknowledged their attraction, he couldn't stop thinking of getting physical with her.

'It's company policy that the head curator accompany the CEO to the yearly fund-raiser for the museum. It's a silent auction thing, pretty boring by all accounts, and, seeing as your cousin can't make it and you're filling in her tours, you'll need to step up. Think you can handle it?'

'No worries.'

She sagged in relief and he chuckled.

'Let me guess. You thought I was going to ask you to clean Steggy.'

Her eyebrows creased into a cute frown. 'Steggy?'

'The stegosaurus skeleton in the entry foyer. You know, that pile of old bones you walk past every day?'

'Oh, that.' She waved her hand as if the priceless dinosaur exhibit were nothing. 'No, I thought you were about to ask me to do something much worse.'

'What's that?'

'Wear those standard-issue flatties most of the staff wear.'

She wrinkled her nose and pursed her lips in a delightful pout as he clamped down the urge to kiss it away. 'Have you really looked at them? They're hideous.'

Shaking his head, he laughed. 'Why do I get the feeling that working with you after this enlightening little chat is going to drive me insane?'

Those entirely too kissable lips eased into a teasing smile as she leaned forward, creating a cleavage a Playboy bunny would be proud of.

'Don't worry. Whatever you're feeling, rest assured it works both ways.'

That was exactly what he was afraid of.

CHAPTER SEVEN

BETH shoved the welding goggles up onto her head, shucked off her protective gloves and wiped a grimy hand over her forehead, cursing under her breath as she stared at her latest creation in disgust.

The twisted pieces of iron resembled overcooked spaghetti rather than the spoked wheel she was aiming for and though most of her pieces were avant-garde this was taking it to extremes.

She'd never had a problem concentrating before. Then again, she'd never had a guy like Aidan Voss interested in her before, let alone been confident enough to admit it.

Guys liked to play games. They didn't do honesty well and they sure didn't verbalise how they were feeling, yet he'd been man enough to listen to what she had to say *and* confirm her suspicions. He fancied her. Hopefully, he fancied the pants off her.

The mere thought set her hands trembling and her insides throbbing and she pushed away from her workbench, knowing she couldn't mould a mud pie let alone metal, the way her hands shook.

Something had shifted between them at Brunetti's, something indefinable, and it had left her wary.

She could party and flirt and laugh her way through any situation, particularly where a good-looking guy was involved, but, now Aidan had admitted he liked her, suddenly the underlying attraction between them wasn't so light-hearted any more.

Now she had to accompany him to a work function, which was all perfectly legitimate and above board, except for one teensy-weensy fact: she didn't want it to be.

She wanted to go on a date with him. She wanted to flirt and tease and encourage that gorgeous smile of his till they were so hot for each other they had no option but to explore this attraction—all the way.

Work function...

Groaning, she switched off the welder and stood, clasping her hands and stretching overhead, letting her head loll forward before rolling the kinks out of it.

Giving Lana an abbreviated version of events was going to be stress-inducing enough without the normal muscle tension that accompanied her beloved metal sculpting.

Casting one last look at the heap of junk she'd managed to construct in the hope of getting her mind off things—or one particularly sexy thing—she picked up her mobile and punched in number one on the auto-dial.

Predictably, Lana answered on the second ring.

'Hey, cuz. It's me.'

'Hi, Beth. How's it going?'

'Good.'

She deliberately turned her back on her disastrous sculpture, an instant reminder of exactly how things were going: a twisted, jumbled mess. 'How's the ankle?'

'Coming along, I guess, but not quickly enough for my liking. How are things at the museum?'

She squeezed the bridge of her nose, hoping she could pull this off. If Lana got one whiff of the situation she'd got into, her cousin would ditch the crutches and hop all the way to Beth's warehouse apartment to give her a swift kick in the butt with her good leg.

Instilling her usual enthusiasm into her voice, she said, 'Fine. I'm still taking tours and it looks like I'll be expanding into some new areas of the museum too.'

'Great. I can't believe you're actually buckling down. I thought being a tour guide would be the last thing you'd want to do.'

'Hey, nothing to it.'

If she didn't count getting hot and bothered every time the boss glanced her way.

'I'm even going to some museum function this weekend so I'm really wowing them.'

'What sort of function?'

Doing her best breezy impression, she plopped onto a nearby sofa and dangled her legs over the end.

'Nothing major, just some silent auction fund-raiser. Apparently it'd be your job to accompany the CEO but you're off your feet so I'm going instead.'

She omitted the part where she wished the CEO would whisk her back to his place afterward and do some very unworklike things with her.

'Uh-oh. You're humming, which means you're nervous, distracted or hyped up about something.'

Beth quickly clamped her lips shut, unaware she'd been indulging in the habit of a lifetime.

'Actually, cuz, none of the above. I just happen to dig that song.'

Damn Aidan Voss for getting under her skin. And into her head. Looked as if he'd crept into her subconscious too.

Lana laughed. 'Thanks for standing in for me at the

function. But remember, it's still work so act professional, okay? I know how much you love a party and you can't afford to fraternise too much, especially if you're accompanying the boss.'

She grimaced, imagining what Lana would think if she knew exactly how much she wanted to fraternise and with whom.

Running a fingernail across the phone to imitate static, she said, 'Sorry, the line's breaking up. Gotta go. Look after that bung leg.'

'Shall do. Have fun at the function, but not too much.'

Beth chuckled, trying to ignore the instant image of Aidan that sprang to mind once she thought of having fun. 'Okay. Bye.'

Hitting the disconnect button, she threw the mobile on the coffee table and sprang up from the sofa.

Maybe she was making too much of a big deal about this. Aidan was just another guy and this was just another function.

Yeah, right.

Sinking back onto her work stool, she yanked her goggles back into place, shoved her hands back into gloves and picked up the welder.

Time to set off some real sparks in more ways than one.

Aidan pulled up outside the derelict old warehouse in the heart of Brunswick and silently cursed the sat nav in his car.

One look at the grubby grey walls, peeling red paint on the solitary door and the deserted street told him he must've punched the wrong address into the whiz-bang gizmo.

So much for satellite navigation, he thought, reaching for the street directory and the piece of paper with Beth's address. However, a brief glance at her bold, flowing script told him he hadn't made a mistake and neither had his car's equipment.

This run-down, eerie warehouse was where she lived.

Shaking his head, he stepped from the car and strode to the door, curiosity lending a spring to his step.

From the minute he'd laid eyes on her he'd known Beth was something else and she'd continued to intrigue him with every passing day. And now this.

With her flair for fashion and sassy attitude he'd pictured her living in some trendy city apartment, living the good life: parties, dancing, café culture. Instead, she chose to live in a dingy Brunswick street, in a place that wouldn't look out of place in a vampire flick.

Brunswick might be one of Melbourne's cosmopolitan inner suburbs, but none of the gloss had reached this place yet. Hitting the intercom button, he waited. And waited. And waited.

He was just about to reach for his mobile when the red door opened with a flourish and his mouth went dry.

'Hey there, Professor. Ready to make tracks?'

It had been worth the wait as he started at the top, admiring her loosely arranged blonde hair half piled on top of her head and allowing his gaze to slide slowly down, taking in the silver shimmery dress skimming her body like liquid metal poured on and ending delightful inches above her knees, the long expanse of bare, bronzed legs and another pair of 'take me' shoes.

Make tracks? Was she kidding? With her in that get-up, a coy smile flirting around her mouth and a mischievous gleam in her eyes, he didn't want to make tracks, he wanted to push his body up against hers, back her into the warehouse and have mind-blowing sex.

Wild, passionate, unrestrained sex, the type of sex he'd been fantasising about ever since he'd caught his first glimpse of her long legs.

'Nice shoes.'

He wrenched his gaze up to meet hers, the faintest hint of

peach beckoning him to close the short distance between them, take hold of her and capture her mouth with every ounce of barely restrained desire pounding through his body.

'We aim to please.'

With a husky laugh that resurrected fond memories of sultry heroines from the classic black and white movies he liked, she shut the door and slipped her hand around his elbow. 'Now, let's go wow these stuffy shirts at the fund-raiser.'

Just like that, some of his good mood evaporated.

Was that how she saw him? As some stuffy professorish type who didn't know how to have fun?

'Am I included in the stuffy-shirt brigade?'

Her eyes glittered with amusement as she laid a hand on his shirt and it took every ounce of will-power not to capture it there and drag the rest of her into his arms.

'You are definitely *not* stuffy-shirt material,' she murmured, her palm smoothing an imaginary crease slowly, sensually, notching up the heat between them and making him grit his teeth with the frustration of not having her naked and panting. 'You're way too adventurous for that.'

'Adventurous, huh?'

'Oh, yeah.'

Her tongue flicked out to moisten her bottom lip, almost undoing his weakening resolve as he reached up and rested a hand on her hip, savouring the feel of hot skin through the slinky fabric of her dress, wishing he could watch it slither down her gorgeous body.

'You're beautiful,' he murmured, trapped in a sensual cocoon of her warm peach fragrance, the spark of desire in her eyes and the secrets in her smile.

'And you're putting some of that much touted charm to very good use.'

Her hand slid downwards to rest on his hip as they stood there for God knew how long, touching each other, locked in each other's stare, their bodies so close but not close enough.

'So am I charming you?'

'Oh, yeah,' she breathed, her eyes conveying a message he was only too happy to read.

'You know we have to go?'

She nodded, tendrils of hair draping her shoulders in shimmering spun gold. 'Maybe you can charm me some more later?'

'It's a promise,' he said, reining in his urge to say, 'To hell with later,' and, taking hold of her hand, he led her to the car.

The faster he did his duty at the fund-raiser, the faster he could get to 'later'.

Beth had never been the clingy type. When she arrived at an event or party she liked to make an entrance. However, the minute she'd stepped out of Aidan's car in front of the elaborate entrance to The Langham hotel and he'd offered her his arm she'd been more than a little grateful for the support.

This evening was going to be chock-full of surprises, starting with Aidan discovering what the lead item in the auction was. And if she hadn't been nervous enough about that, seeing him dressed in a designer tux, compelling smile in place and touching her hand with ease as if he squired flirty females to fancy functions every day of the week would've set her nerves jumping anyway.

She clutched his arm a tad tighter as they entered the foyer, her heels clicking on the highly polished marble as the reflected light from a stunning chandelier momentarily dazzled her. Only slightly more than the sexy man staring at her with a quizzical expression, that was.

'You were humming under your breath.'

'I always hum. Lifelong habit. My dad used to say there's a song for every occasion. Guess he was right.'

There was a slight pause and he steadied her as they stepped off the top of an escalator. 'Used to?'

'He died when I was eighteen.'

Almost to the day. It was as if he'd waited till she could legally do everything for herself before pegging out. Pity he hadn't done a thing for her emotionally while he'd still been alive.

She expected a trite 'I'm sorry.' Instead, he said, 'Do you miss him?'

Good question. Shame she didn't have the faintest clue how to answer.

'I guess. My mum died when I was six and my dad went a bit crazy after that. He dragged me around from town to town, either trying to escape memories or create new ones. We were close for a while until I got sick of living like a gypsy and he didn't want to hear my complaints. He dumped me with my cousin and her dad for six months of every year and I loved it, but then he'd breeze into Melbourne again and yank me away, hitting the road while all I wanted to do was stay put. He just never understood.'

'Families, huh?'

She saw the pity in his eyes even as he tried to make light of her admission and it annoyed her.

She didn't need his pity.

She didn't need anyone's pity.

She'd done a fine job taking care of herself all these years and apart from Lana she knew better than to depend on anyone, especially some guy who thought he could get around her with smouldering grey eyes and a sexy smile.

'The way you said families, sounds like you have a tale of

your own to tell,' she said, determined to deflect his attention away from her morbid past.

She noticed the slight tightening around the corners of his mouth, the tense jaw muscle near his ears, though his smile didn't waver.

'Not much to tell, I'm afraid. My folks are both historians. I travelled the world with them while I was young before dad took over as CEO of the museum. He ran it for twenty-five years before asking me to step in temporarily.'

'Keeping it all in the family,' she said, surprised by the flicker of bitterness in his eyes.

'Something like that.'

They'd reached the entrance to the ballroom where the auction was being held and a round of introductions to a group of people she had no hope of remembering stalled any further probing on her part.

For that was exactly what she'd been about to do: delve into Aidan's past. He had a story to tell, she could sense it. What better way to gain insight into the guy than by discovering his background? Besides, it was much more fun than dwelling on her family life—or lack of.

'Want to check out what's on offer?'

'I already did.'

Her gaze perused the length and breadth of him before sending him a coquettish look from beneath her lashes.

He laughed, a low rumble of pure joy that sent a thrill through her. 'See anything you fancy?'

'Sure do,' she murmured, mentally moving his butt to the top of her very own grope-able list. 'Though I'm not sure if it's in my price range?'

The fine hairs on the nape of her neck stood to attention as he leaned closer, his breath fanning out against her cheek.

'There's only one way to find out. Why don't you put in a bid? You never know, you might get lucky.'

Everything faded away—the muted light from wall sconces dancing off sequinned designer dresses, the soft classical music filtering from a high-tech sound system, the drone of voices from a thousand-odd people—as his lips brushed her cheek in the lightest of touches, so light she could've imagined it. Or willed it, more likely.

Caught in the heat of his stare, the spicy blackcurrant undertones of his aftershave invading her senses, she struggled not to close the short gap between them and do what she'd wanted to do since their first memorable kiss—a repeat performance.

'Get lucky, huh? I'm counting on it.'

Her words came out on a whisper as his fingertips slid up her arm, skimming her bare skin like the touch of the flimsiest butterfly wings taking flight.

'If this evening wasn't so damn important for the museum I'd say let's blow this place.'

Stifling a sigh of disappointment at his CEO conscientiousness, she tapped his cheek lightly. 'Don't worry. The night is young.'

He sent her a scorching look that set her body tingling all the way down to her metallic blue toenails poking from her Gary Castle silver spiked stilettos, but before he could say anything further a guy bearing a striking resemblance to Harrison Ford in *Indiana Jones*, complete with battered hat, bore down on them and practically dragged Aidan away.

Grinning at his pained expression, she sent him a jaunty wave and headed for the front of the room where a roped-off area kept curious buyers away from the more expensive items.

Professional pride filled her as she stared at her latest

triumph, a mini version of the Sydney Opera House, her very own interpretation of the iconic landmark.

'The least you could've done is rescue me. You're supposed to be supporting me, remember?'

Beth turned to Aidan, surprised he'd returned to her side so quickly.

'I didn't think you needed rescuing. After all, don't you CEO types need to mingle and schmooze and generally suck up to people?'

He frowned, as if her teasing hit too close to home.

'You're right. CEOs probably do have to do that sort of thing, which is why I'd rather spend the bulk of the evening with you.'

A warm glow filled her. Apart from the steamy attraction between them, she genuinely liked him and what had looked at first glance like a novel way to secure her lease and help Lana out was fast turning into something far more important with a certain scary twang in the vicinity of her heart, the type of twang that said she could seriously dig this guy if she let go.

Flustered by the uncharacteristic surge of emotion clogging her throat, she gestured towards her sculpture.

'What do you think of this piece?'

He screwed up his eyes, tilted his head first right, then left, before taking a step back and repeating the process. 'Not my sort of thing. Too modern.'

The tender emotion of a moment ago melted away as she absorbed the critical look on his face and came to a startling realisation.

His opinion mattered to her.

He'd hurt her.

Which could only mean one thing: she could be falling for him.

Madness, considering they wanted different things out of

life: confirmed nomad versus wannabe homebody. A match made in heaven: not.

Desperate to ignore the surge of panic telling her to make a run for it while she still could, she forced a laugh.

'Of course it's too modern for you, considering you've spent half your life rummaging in the dirt looking for old stuff.'

Something in her tone must have alerted him to the fact she wasn't as unaffected by his opinion as she'd like to be, for he captured her chin in his hands and tilted it up gently until she had no option but to stare into his disgustingly gorgeous eyes.

'What's up?'

'Nothing.'

She dropped her gaze before he read the lie there, only to be confronted by his equally gorgeous lips, the lips that felt exceptionally good plastered against her own.

'This isn't the time or place,' he said, in a voice like smooth velvet as he skimmed his thumb along her bottom lip for a moment before letting go as if he'd been burned. 'But, trust me, if you look at me like that later tonight I won't be held responsible for my actions.'

Grateful they'd slipped back into flirting mode, she quirked an eyebrow and tapped his chest with a French manicured fingernail.

'Haven't you heard? Being responsible all the time is highly overrated.'

Flecks of speckled cobalt flared amidst the dreamy grey depths of his eyes as a confident smile curved his lips. 'I'm all for forgetting my responsibilities for a night.'

Splaying her palm on his chest, she absorbed the heat radiating through his dress shirt before sliding her hand down and tucking it around his elbow as if that had been her intention all along.

'And I'm all for being the one responsible for you forgetting. But don't we have an auction to attend first?'

Muttering a curse, he tucked her hand closer and headed into the ballroom at a half-run.

She laughed. 'If you're in a hurry because you can't wait to get me alone later, I like the way you think.'

He stopped dead and she bumped into his side, relishing the all-too-brief contact of one half of his body slamming against hers.

'I'm hoping you'll like a lot more than that.'

He slipped a protective arm around her waist as his smouldering gaze sent a thrill of anticipation through her. 'In fact, I'm counting on it.'

Beth couldn't think for a moment, what with his hand nestled comfortably around her waist, his thumb strumming back and forth, and the intent in his eyes notching up her excitement levels to unbearable.

Moistening her bottom lip with her tongue, and enjoying the fleeting tortured expression that flickered across his face, she dropped her voice to a whisper.

'The faster you bid, the faster we get to the good stuff.'

With a muffled groan he released her. 'Come on, quit dawdling.'

She chuckled, the confident sound of a woman who knew what she liked in a man and how to get it, as Aidan all but dragged her into the ballroom in a fair imitation of a sedate sprint.

CHAPTER EIGHT

'You should've told me.'

Beth unlocked her front door and pushed it open, flinging a mischievous look over her shoulder with a toss of her silky blonde hair. 'Why? I knew you'd find out soon enough.'

Shaking his head, Aidan followed her into the cavernous warehouse, hoping the inside was a lot more inviting than the bleak exterior.

'You got that right.' He blinked as she flicked on switches, flooding a suspended wooden walkway in light. 'Unfortunately, I get to find out that my newest wannabe tour guide is actually a star sculptor when I see her name on the programme, and how much her art is worth rather than hearing it from the sculptor herself.'

She chuckled, the throaty, full-on laugh he'd grown way too fond of way too quickly.

'It's your fault. I was going to tell you before you wrinkled your uppity nose at my best work in ages and said it was "too modern".'

His mouth twitched as he feigned indignation. 'There's nothing uppity about my nose and I definitely didn't sound like Barry White on steroids when I said it was too modern.'

Unfortunately, he thought, considering most women were

into that soul-deep crooning-voice thing, as he followed her down the walkway before stepping down a small flight of stairs into a room the size of a small aircraft hangar.

She laughed and crooked a finger over her shoulder, beckoning him to follow. As if he needed to be asked twice.

'Some place.'

He did a three-sixty, taking in the eclectic mix of rippled steel cciling, white-washed stone walls, honey-coloured wooden slat blinds over monstrous windows and the largest, brightest splashes of paint passing as pictures hanging on the walls at various spots throughout the warehouse.

'I like it.' She headed into a tiny kitchenette at odds with the size of the rest of the place. 'What would you like to drink?'

'Coffee's fine. Black, one sugar, thanks.'

He headed over to a spotlit corner featuring a giant Japanese screen inlaid with the finest mother-of-pearl cherry-blossom motif. It was a work of art and he couldn't help but run his fingertips over the exquisite work.

He missed the fieldwork, missed the excitement of searching, the thrill of discovering ancient items of beauty. Things like this screen were made for the world to appreciate yet the closest he got these days was staring at priceless pieces behind the glass of a museum cabinet with the rest of the public rather than touching and feeling and experiencing the sheer rush of finding a beautiful artefact.

He couldn't wait to get back out there and the sooner Abe returned from his R & R, the sooner he could get back to the digs.

'If you like the screen, wait till you get a load of what's behind it.'

She joined him, handing over a mug of steaming coffee before stepping around the screen and jerking her head to indicate he should follow.

'This is where I work. Though I guess it's not really your thing, being so *modern* and all.'

'Give a guy a break,' he said, sipping at his coffee, wondering whether the jolt of energy coursing through his veins came from the caffeine rush or the sight of Beth picking up pliers and a shiny sheet of steel, caressing the metal with the kind of touch she'd reserve for a lover.

'I'll think about it.'

She shot him an impudent smile before gripping the metal with the pliers and twisting it into a star with origami-like precision.

'You're very talented.'

He drained his coffee and placed the mug on a sideboard before joining her at the workbench. 'Why didn't you tell me about all this? Really?'

Her hands stilled, the pliers looking surprisingly delicate resting in her palm despite their size and function as she raised her eyes to meet his.

'Because it wasn't relevant to my job and that's what you've been pretty focussed on every time we've talked before our chat at Brunetti's.'

She was right.

She was brash, funny, exuberant and obviously thought he was the opposite considering her nickname for him. She thought he was a pedantic workaholic who was too focussed on the museum. Sadly, she was absolutely spot on. He never used to be that guy, but he was these days and for what? To prove something to a man who probably wouldn't notice if he danced naked on top of the Sphinx?

When she didn't respond, he sat down on a stool next to her and picked up a miniature wrought-iron basket. 'Being your boss and all that entails hasn't given you a very good impression of me, huh?'

She gnawed on her bottom lip and he struggled to ignore the surge of lust at how much he'd like to do the same.

'Actually, you've been pretty great about everything.'

'But you think I'm judgemental.'

Hell, he'd probably reacted to her work exactly how she'd thought he would. Though she didn't say the words, he remembered her disappointment when he'd commented on her show-stopper at the auction before she'd masked it with her usual quick wit.

'Not really,' she muttered, lacking total conviction, and he drifted towards a nearby bookcase constructed from twisted metal and glass, grasping at a change of subject.

Scanning the shelves, he was surprised by the strange mix of anatomy and psychology texts next to classic literature.

'Bit of light reading?'

She swivelled to face him, wariness clouding her eyes. 'Just some stuff I read in my teens while trying to figure out what I wanted to do with my life.'

His eyebrows shot up. 'You read *Gray's Anatomy* in your teens?'

She shrugged and fiddled with the pliers, twisting a metal sliver into a pretzel. 'I was gifted.'

She dropped the bombshell in the same monotone a kid might use to request a peanut-butter sandwich.

'Let me get this straight. Your IQ is off the charts, you could be anything you want and you choose to do that?'

He knew it was the wrong thing to say the instant the pliers sheered off and sliced the metal clean in two.

Damn it, he usually weighed his words as carefully as his decisions, but somehow her announcement had thrown him more than discovering the wrought-iron impression of the Sydney Opera House at the auction tonight was her creation.

Picking up another sheet of metal, she resumed her twisting with the pliers and he had the distinct feeling she was wishing it were his head.

'I like what I do. I like being creative,' she said, her voice glacial, her eyes shooting green fire as she stabbed at the metal, making a giant hole for goodness knew what reason. 'I don't like being judged by the size of my brain.'

She paused to give a particularly vicious twist to the metal to the point where it bent and contorted to breaking-point. 'And I really, really don't like some judgemental jackass like you belittling what I do.'

She was right, again. He didn't take her job seriously and hadn't from the first moment he'd learned the truth tonight.

Mentally kicking himself for being such a moron, he crossed the room to stand in front of her, willing her to look at him again, to pay as much attention to him as she was to the bizarre creation in her hands.

'You know what I like?'

'What?'

She lifted her head a fraction, enough for him to see her frown while her body language—folded arms, tense shoulders, slight lean away from him—screamed hands off.

Yeah, as if he could do that.

'You,' he said softly, cupping her chin, using the gentlest of pressure to lift her face towards his, hoping she'd listen to what he had to say after the way he'd blundered through things the last few minutes. 'I like you. I'm sorry I offended you. You caught me off guard, that's all.'

Her compressed lips softened a tad but she didn't lose the frown. 'It still doesn't change the fact you think I'm wasting my time being a metal sculptor rather than using my brain for something more worthwhile. Like an archaeologist perhaps? Or maybe a brain surgeon? Or a rocket scientist?'

She snapped her fingers. 'I know, maybe I should be the world's greatest tour guide.'

Suddenly, her frown vanished, accompanied by a twitching of the corners of her lush mouth. 'Oh, that's right. I already am.'

To his amazement, she laughed, a laugh that echoed in the cavernous warehouse, bouncing off the walls until it seemed to envelop him with her natural spontaneity and warmth.

'So I take it I'm forgiven for being a conservative jerk who can't think before he speaks?'

'There's nothing conservative about you.'

Her eyes widened to large green pools as his hand slid from under her chin to rest at the nape of her neck, as if she anticipated his next move would be to draw her closer and kiss her senseless.

'Just in case, I think it's time to shake things up a bit, to show you exactly how non-conservative I can be.'

Aidan didn't know who made the first move but suddenly the short space between him and a handful of luscious woman vanished in an instant as they lunged at each other.

'Never knew you could lighten up this much, Professor.' She gasped as he slid his hands over her shoulders, pushing down the flimsy straps holding up her shimmery, barely there dress as he'd been yearning to do all evening.

'There's a lot you don't know about me, Fancy Feet,' he murmured, savouring the feel of silky-soft skin beneath his fingertips, blazing a trail with his lips where his hands had just been.

A weird sound somewhere between a snort and a laugh erupted near his ear. 'Fancy Feet?'

He raised his head from the creamy skin of her neck reluctantly, muttering a curse.

'Not the most romantic endearment you've ever heard, I bet.'

She smiled, a sensuous upward curving of her lips that had him dying to cover them with his own.

'I've heard better. Then again, it is original.'

'It's those damn shoes you keep wearing.'

He pointed to yet another sexy ensemble designed to entice and draw his attention to the perfection of her endless legs. 'How's a guy supposed to not ogle your sensational legs when you draw attention to them with shoes like that?'

He slid his arms around her waist, pulling her close until she couldn't mistake the bulge in his pants for anything other than what it was: irreversible proof of exactly how much he desired her.

She smirked and wound her arms around his neck, pulling his head down towards her. 'Now that we've established how much we like each other with the nickname thing and how much you like my shoes, where were we?'

'Right here.'

He settled his lips over hers, more than a little disconcerted at how right it felt.

As if he'd finally come home.

As if this was the type of woman he could get used to having around for longer than his usual few dates.

But that could never be.

He'd almost given up everything once before and he could never settle in one place again, no matter how much he wanted to or for whom.

He deepened the kiss, pure, unadulterated lust shooting through him as she matched him thrust for thrust, her tongue winding around his, teasing, tasting, taking as much as she gave.

He groaned as her hands grabbed his butt, hanging on as if she couldn't get enough while her mouth left his only to nibble her way across his jaw to his ear where she bit down, hard enough to brand him as hers, soft enough to leave him begging for more.

'Bedroom?' he managed to grit out as she slid a hand around from his butt to cup his erection, sending the blood roaring through his head as she shifted her hand up and down the length of him.

'Now, now, where's your famous adventurous spirit?'

She sent a pointed look at the plush red rug beneath their feet and he grinned, more than eager to dispense with the wasted seconds it would take to reach her bedroom.

'I like the way you think.'

He tugged on the zip holding up the silver sheath, smiling when it gave a satisfying hiss and the dress pooled in a glittering heap at her feet.

'That's a mighty confident grin,' she murmured, not in the least embarrassed as his gaze left her face to slide downwards, his breath catching at the sight of her beautiful breasts. Full. Round. Exquisite.

Unable to keep his hands off them a second longer, he cupped them, savouring their lushness, skimming a thumb over each pale brown nipple. 'That's because I'm guessing we're a sure thing right about now?'

'Good guess.'

She drew his belt out of his trousers' loops inch by slow inch, deliberately brushing against his erection with every move. Torturing him, teasing him, her touch driving him slowly but surely crazy.

He usually liked to take things slow, to draw out the pleasure, but with every tantalising touch he knew he'd combust if he didn't follow this base instinct and have fast and furious sex with this feisty woman who could turn him on with the barest hint of a twinkle in her incredible eyes.

As if she sensed his need the next few moments were a blur of fast hands, flying garments and clashing mouths as they repeatedly kissed while tearing each others' clothes off, the air filled with her soft pants and his heavy groans.

'At last,' he murmured as she stood before him, naked, glorious, her suddenly shy smile hitting him where he least expected it: his heart.

His *heart*?

Hell, it really had been way too long since he'd had sex. Since when did he let himself feel anything beyond job satisfaction, let alone emotion?

Emotions were wasted. They built hopes, fuelled dreams, before disintegrating into the dust he dug through. He'd learned it as a boy, had had it confirmed as a man and there was no way he'd let Beth get too close no matter how much she captivated him.

'Come on.'

She tugged him down to the rug and he quickly banished his thoughts to concentrate on the task at hand and that was losing his mind with the woman who turned him on with a simple smile.

Beth moaned as Aidan's lips trailed down her neck, hard, insistent, creating heat and sending rivers of mind-numbing need flooding through her body.

'Oh!' She arched upwards as his mouth found her nipple, sucking, nipping, teasing her with his skilful tongue while his hands were free to roam south, skimming her belly before gently spreading her thighs.

'Am I going too fast for you?'

He lifted his head as she let out another hearty moan and she laughed, shaking her head.

'What would you do if I said not fast enough?'

His eyes darkened to pewter as his lips curved into a naughty smile, a smile loaded with wicked promise.

'I'd do this.'

With a fast move she'd associate with an X-rated star rather than a CEO he'd flipped her around, his hot breath fanning against her stomach and bringing his arousal in her direct line of vision.

'Slick, Professor, very slick,' she murmured, a second before he placed his mouth against her throbbing centre, sending sparks of electricity shooting through her body in little bursts of pleasure.

'Fast enough for you?'

He spread her further apart, his tongue finding her clitoris with unerring accuracy, licking at her, flicking her in quick little darting movements designed to send her into orbit in the blink of an eye.

'Oh, yeah,' she said through gritted teeth, wondering if there was a world record for the fastest orgasm ever, sure she was about to beat it with the help of one very sexy guy.

He paused, sending her a scorching glance. 'We've done it your way for a while, now we do it mine.'

She made a tiny mewl of disappointment, her pelvis making a small unconscious thrust up towards his mouth, shamelessly begging for more.

'You may like things fast, but we staid museum types prefer it slow. Real slow.'

He dipped his head to lick her once, twice. Long, drawn out sweeps with his tongue, which had her biting her lower lip to stop from crying out.

'Slow is good too,' she managed to get out before he picked up where he'd left off, though this time at a much slower pace, which drove her wilder than before.

Closing her eyes, she gave in to the sensations bombarding her, making more noise than was surely polite for a first time with a guy but not giving a damn.

She was blinded with mindless need, and her head dropped forward, only to be nudged by the hard evidence of what her rather shameless noises were doing to him.

'Payback time…' She leaned forward a fraction to take him in her mouth, enjoying the tortured groan he let out as she licked him with the same fervour he was inflicting on her.

'Too much,' he muttered, picking up where he'd left off for a second, driving her to the brink of losing control.

'On the contrary, not nearly enough.' She raised her head to send him a seductive smile.

She'd never felt this empowered, this confident and it had everything to do with the guy about to send her to the moon and back with the best orgasm of her life.

However, before she could resume her ministrations, Aidan did some weird circular thing with his tongue once, twice and she shattered, her inner muscles clenching, her outer muscles dissolving as she came apart on a loud moan.

Smiling, he shimmied up to join her, caressing her cheek with an unbearable tenderness in his eyes. 'Please tell me you don't live in this place without a neighbour within coo-ee because you regularly make sounds like that.'

'Fine, I won't tell you.'

She planted a lip-smacking kiss on his mouth while sliding her hand down the hard planes of his stomach, savouring the feel of smooth skin, the rasp of hair below his navel arrowing downwards.

'But just for the record, I chose this location for the workshop space, not for the lack of nosy neighbours who might have a hankering to listen to noises that don't occur very often anyway.'

Considering he'd just given her the orgasm to end all orgasms, the triumphant, gloating, all-male glint in his eyes didn't surprise her. He was good, damn good, and knew it too.

'Good to know,' he said, his hands stroking her back in slow, sweeping movements until she almost purred like a cat, a well-sated cat.

'Now, before you get too conceited—and, yes, the noise I made definitely corresponds with how amazingly talented you are with your tongue—it's time to return the favour.'

Grinning like the smug male he was following the ego-trip she'd just sent him on, he grabbed his trousers, withdrew a condom from his wallet and sheathed himself quickly before laying back, hands folded under his neck, elbows out, the epitome of a guy who knew he was smoking-hot and how badly she wanted him.

'I'm all yours. Go ahead, do your worst.'

'That's some challenge,' she murmured, straddling him in a second, enjoying the desperate look that flickered across his face as she brushed his erection with her slick entrance.

'Lucky for you, my worst also happens to be my best.' She slid downwards, inch by torturous inch until he filled her completely, revelling in the feel of him inside her, the anticipation building all over again as she began to move up and down.

'You're incredible,' he ground out as he grasped her waist, matching her pace, thrusting up as she slid down, his smouldering gaze not leaving hers.

Beth always had to have the last word and could usually come up with a quip in a second. However, with his every thrust she coiled tighter inside, the tension rebuilding until she could do little but hang on for the ride.

'Oh, yeah!'

His guttural groan heralded her own release as stars danced before her eyes and she collapsed on top of him, her body turning into a sensual puddle of stimulated nerve endings and mushy muscles.

Shifting slightly beneath her, he cradled her head, lifting it until he could look directly into her eyes.

'You just blew my mind,' he said, slanting a slow burning kiss across her lips, the kind of kiss that had her wishing he'd be sticking around for longer than a few months.

'Same here.'

Smiling, he kissed her again and again, soul-drugging, toe-curling, mind-blowing kisses designed to take her on an erotic journey to a record number of orgasms in one night.

Humming the faintest strains of Marvin Gaye's 'Sexual Healing' under her breath, she gave herself over to enjoying what promised to be the best night's sex of her life.

CHAPTER NINE

'WHAT'S going on?'

Beth stopped chopping onions and dashed a hand across her teary eyes, squinting at her cousin propped in the kitchen doorway.

'I'm making you my world-famous lasagne, that's what. Personally, I think you're taking this whole invalid thing a tad far. I'm betting you ditch the crutches the moment I'm out the door and dance around here naked.'

Lana quirked an eyebrow and stared down at her baggy brown cords, shapeless beige sweater and Doc Martens, her usual daggy stay-at-home garb. 'You think?'

Beth laughed, wishing Lana would let her spice up her wardrobe a little. It might help her to loosen up, act her age, have a little fun, maybe go the whole hog and find a guy. 'Well, maybe not. Now, vamoose. You have a master chef at work here.'

Lana shook her head and hobbled towards the breakfast bar. 'Sorry. Not leaving till you tell me what's up.'

'All this lazing around has given you an overactive imagination. There's nothing wrong.'

Beth resumed dicing, needing to keep her hands busy and her mind focussed on getting the recipe just right; anything to keep her mind off the extremely X-rated fantasies—though they could officially be classed as memories now—of Aidan.

Lana picked up a wooden spoon and banged it on the side of a stainless-steel cookie container. 'Spill it. You only ever make lasagne as comfort food, so give over. Something's wrong.'

Turning away from Lana's probing stare, Beth winced at what she was about to do.

Considering her cousin would have to work with Aidan once her ankle healed, it was only fair she told her the truth. Besides, Lana had been her confidante, best friend and sister rolled into one for ever and she was busting to tell her what had gone down—literally—with Aidan.

Rinsing her hands under the cold tap and drying off, she turned to face Lana, drew out a kitchen chair and pointed to it.

'You better sit down. I have a feeling you're going to need to when you finish hearing this.'

Concern crossed Lana's face in an instant. 'Are you okay? It's nothing serious?'

Gnawing at her bottom lip, she dropped into the chair opposite Lana and said, 'Depends on your definition of serious. If you think sleeping with the boss is serious, well, then, it's—'

'You did *what*?'

Lana sat bolt upright so quickly one of her crutches toppled and slammed against the floor with a bang.

'It's no big deal, really,' Beth hurried on, more than a little intimidated by the appalled look on her cousin's face. 'We've had this flirting thing going on from the start and we kinda got carried away after that fund-raiser and—'

Lana shook her head and held up her hands. 'Whoa! Tell me this is yet another example of your warped sense of humour. Tell me you didn't really sleep with Aidan Voss.'

Beth tried to keep a straight face and failed. She couldn't, because the instant Lana mentioned Aidan's name she couldn't keep the smile off her face.

'Okay, I didn't really sleep with Aidan Voss…considering there wasn't much sleep involved.'

Lana groaned and dropped her head in her hands. 'This is insane. He's your boss, *our* boss!'

Banishing thoughts of how fabulous the little sleeping she'd had with Aidan had been, she sobered up for her cousin's sake.

'Look, it's not that bad. We're both consenting adults, it's not really going anywhere and once he finishes his stint at the museum it'll all be forgotten.'

Lana's head snapped up as she pinned her with an accusatory glance. 'You think?'

Beth dropped her gaze, preferring to trace the chocolate brown and aqua circles on the fifties tablecloth rather than face the judgement in Lana's eyes.

Knowing Lana wouldn't buy her best innocent look—she never had, all those times Beth had swapped book reports, 'borrowed' her best jewellery, pilfered the last of her favourite chocolate bar—she tried one on for size anyway.

'Look, we laid out the ground rules. This isn't going to affect our working relationship at all. I made sure he understands that.'

'All very nice in theory, but have you seriously thought this through? What can happen to your job if you botch this?'

'Settle down, cuz. Nothing's going to happen. I'm working my butt off at the museum to keep my job and everything's cool.'

Extremely cool, considering how they'd blown each other's minds last night.

After several deep breaths, which restored her colour, Lana

said, 'Okay, you seem to have a handle on the job side of things.' She tapped a split fingernail against her bottom lip before shouting, 'But honestly, what on earth possessed you to sleep with him?'

'Would you believe the devil made me do it?'

Beth couldn't help her response and she sure couldn't control the smile tweaking her lips.

Ever since they were kids she'd been making Lana laugh, trying to lighten up her serious cousin, trying to make her see that life wasn't all textbooks and museums.

Thankfully, Lana was usually a good sport and her tight-lipped, grim expression softened a moment later.

'You're nuts, you know that?'

Beth shrugged and picked up the pitcher of iced green tea she'd set out earlier, pouring them both a generous glass. 'Like you didn't already know.'

Lana accepted the proffered glass, the rim barely hiding her growing smile.

'You actually slept with Voss the Boss,' she murmured, shaking her head before taking a healthy slurp.

'And you're actually lightening up enough to call him that?'

She met Lana's bemused glance and they burst out laughing.

'I guess it's pointless me asking how good he was?'

'You can ask, I just won't tell you.'

Beth hoped the instant heat flooding her body at the memory of her night with Aidan didn't make it to her cheeks. 'Besides, you're the workaholic. Think how awkward it could be at your first staff meeting, trying to maintain a professional front when you know how long his—'

'Point taken.'

Lana almost snorted the remainder of her tea before her smile faded and she leaned forward, pushing her glasses back up her nose and reverting to her usual serious mode. 'Just be careful, okay?'

'Of what?'

Lana paused, as if searching for the right words, before blowing out a long breath that sent her scraggly fringe heavenward.

'You date a lot of guys and pretend to be the ultimate party girl, but I know for a fact you don't sleep with many of them. And I've got to say I'm pretty surprised you're even interested in Aidan considering he's probably not your type.'

Beth frowned, still none the wiser about her cousin's warning. Was she trying to tell her to take care of her own feelings or Aidan's?

'You're being as clear as mud. Come on, spit it out. I'm a big girl. I can take it.'

Concern flashed in Lana's eyes before she blurted, 'If Aidan's reputation as one of the world's best archaeologists is accurate he won't be staying around for long. He'll be heading off into the wild blue yonder faster than you can say palaeontology.'

'And your point is?'

Though she knew and didn't need her cousin to articulate what she'd been thinking since last night. She wouldn't have slept with Aidan unless he meant something to her and now that she had she couldn't help but think beyond that one, incredible night.

She'd craved a stable home her whole life, had yearned to stay in the one place and build a family of her own she could depend on, which meant she had pretty lousy judgement considering she'd just fallen for a guy who'd been blunt about his fever for travelling the world.

Lana topped up her glass and took a long sip before answering. 'We both know you want a long-term relationship. And we both know why.'

Her heart sank. She should be on a high after last night. Instead, here she was playing twenty questions with her nosy cousin and having to suffer her amateur psychobabble to boot.

'This has nothing to do with my dad.'

She kept her tone deliberately flat, downing another top-up and leaping from her chair. 'Now, I really have to finish this bolognese sauce if you want to eat any time this century.'

Lana wouldn't push.

She knew it; Lana knew it.

It had always been the way with them: Beth the confident, outspoken one, Lana the shy, retiring one who gave her opinion but wouldn't force the issue no matter how right she was.

'Fine. I just care about you.'

Lana's soft-spoken words hung in the air and Beth blinked several times, grateful her back was turned.

'Right back at you, cuz,' she said in a fake, perky falsetto, resuming her chopping at a frantic pace in an attempt to drown out any further forays into topics she'd rather not discuss.

Pity she couldn't drown out her thoughts, especially the main one centred around one very sexy boss and the strange urge to do something completely out of character…like fall head over heels for him despite the fact he had wanderlust in his veins.

Beth found herself humming again on Aidan's doorstep before quickly silencing her vocal cords.

She'd never been this nervous and it was all Lana's fault. So he'd invited her to dinner at his place? No big deal.

However, ever since Lana had planted the idea of Aidan about to do a runner in her head she'd been as fidgety as her cousin that time she'd offered to dust her precious sake cup collection.

She didn't do a lot of forward thinking as a rule. She always lived life to the fullest, making the most of every precious second. Losing her mum had taught her that.

But her dad had taught her, however inadvertently, the value of staying in one location long enough to build a place to call her own, to value dependence on those closest to you, to have a base, the one stable place you could head to for refuge no matter what happened.

The only time she'd had something like that was when she'd stayed with Lana and her uncle, those few, brief, precious months every year when her dad would feel guilty for dragging her around the countryside and give in to her pleading. It had never lasted.

Now here she was, getting in deeper by the day with a guy who'd up and leave any time, a guy who already had a first love: his job.

The door opened and she fixed a smile on her face, more than a little disconcerted a family of butterflies had taken up residence in her stomach. Worse, they took flight the second she caught sight of Aidan in casual gear for the first time, wearing a navy T-shirt, faded denim and a sexy smile.

'Hey, Beth. Any trouble finding the place?'

Dragging her gaze away from his chest, which appeared so much broader in soft cotton than the stiff business shirts he usually wore, she sent him a flirtatious glance from beneath her lashes.

'I'm here, aren't I?'

'You sure are.'

She propped in the doorway, enjoying his leisurely

perusal, wondering if he approved of her outfit as much as she did his.

'Nice shoes.'

He sent her a sizzling look that said the Marc Jacobs avocado satin ankle-tie-ups were a hit.

'Enough with the shoes fetish already.'

She rolled her eyes in mock exasperation as she slid past him, planting a casual kiss on his cheek as if having dinner with the guy she'd had sensational sex with the night before was something she did every day.

'Anything you say, Fancy Feet.'

She smiled, still not quite believing he'd given her a nickname. He'd surprised her on many levels, especially with the inventive talents he'd exhibited last night.

'Something smells great.'

She inhaled deeply as she followed him up a short hallway and into the most bizarre kitchen she'd ever seen with its old-versus-new motif: ultra-mod stainless-steel appliances clashing oddly with an old-fashioned dresser covered in Wedgwood plates, the black granite bench-tops out of place next to an old Aga stove.

'It's one of my foolproof recipes, from a limited repertoire, I might add,' he said, lifting a pot to release a fragrant aroma of lemongrass and coconut into the air, which made her mouth water. 'Hope you like Thai chicken curry.'

'Love it.'

She slid the bottle of chilled white wine she'd brought out of her bag and plonked it on the granite-topped bench before pulling up a stool, afraid of how much she liked his domestic side, the comfortable atmosphere between them and how much she'd love it to exist beyond this night.

'I'll just pop the rice on, then we can relax in the other

room,' he threw over his shoulder, looking way too efficient as he measured out the jasmine rice, the water, added a pinch of salt and set the lot to boil.

Apart from lasagne she could barely make a cup of tea and adding culinary expertise to Aidan's growing repertoire of talents wasn't helping the stayer-versus-fling argument echoing through her head.

She wanted him to be a stayer; he was definitely a fling type of guy. What if they couldn't come to an agreement? What then?

'There, all done.'

He wiped his hands on a tea-towel hanging on the oven door handle, giving her a prime view of his butt as he bent forward. 'Now, for some wine…'

He trailed off as he stood a lot quicker than anticipated and caught her staring at him, a slow smile spreading across his face. 'Or would you prefer something else?'

Ignoring the way her heart pounded at the thought of 'something else', she handed him the bottle of wine.

'As much as I fancy dessert I'll settle for wine now.'

His eyes glittered with fervour as he registered what she meant. Okay, so she hadn't banked on getting horizontal by the end of this evening, but seeing him look at her with potent desire told her exactly how much she was kidding herself.

She had as much chance of resisting him as taking some monotonous desk job somewhere: absolutely none.

She wanted him. Naked. Gloriously naked. Skin on skin. With her.

Beth wasn't sure how long they stayed that way, gazes locked, the heat sizzling between them having little to do with the curry and rice simmering on the stove, but she was the first to break the deadlock before she flung herself over the breakfast bar and tackled him to the floor.

'Interesting place.'

She swivelled on the bar stool away from his assessing stare, willing her heart to stop pounding like a temp with a crush on her first boss.

Though what hope did she have, with Aidan propped against one of the bench-tops, looking sinfully delicious, more so than the chocolate mousse she'd glimpsed when he'd opened the fridge.

'This place belongs to my folks. I'm crashing here while I'm caretaker CEO.'

She couldn't fathom the strange look he got every time he mentioned his family, an almost furtive guilty expression that darkened his eyes with pain.

'Mum wanted the appliances, though goodness knows why as she rarely cooks. As for all the plates and other paraphernalia, she's a hoarder from way back. Collecting old stuff goes with the territory of being a historian.'

Bemused by the cynicism in his voice, she tucked her feet under the stool rung and wriggled till she was comfortable. 'Considering your job you must be into hanging on to old stuff too. What do you collect?'

He paused, sending her a wicked grin that curled her toes. 'Hotties, just like you.'

Twirling a strand of hair around her finger—wishing she could do the same to him—she leaned forward and lowered her voice. 'I'm guessing you're not referring to the ceramic type.'

'You mean like your extensive collection?'

They laughed as Beth wondered how she'd ever thought she could convince him she was conservative enough to do that.

'You know, Lana actually does collect ceramic hot-water bottles.'

'Really?'

She nodded, surprised by the swift stab of jealousy at the sudden interest in his eyes, glad when his gaze dipped to her cleavage briefly before returning to her face, scorching in its intensity.

'Personally, I'm into hotties that collect shoes.'

He pushed off the bench-top, his biceps bunching deliciously as he strode across the kitchen and offered her his hand, his smile giving those damn butterflies in her stomach a new lease of life.

'Come on, I'll give you the grand tour.'

'Is this your less than subtle way of getting me into your bedroom?'

Heat pooled in her belly at the thought as she slipped her hand into his, powerless to resist this sexy guy at his flirting best.

He wiggled his eyebrows suggestively, the action so ludicrously exaggerated she laughed.

'No, it's my way of taking my mind off exactly how hot you are and stopping myself from getting down and dirty with you right here, right now.'

'Oh,' she managed as all the air whooshed out of her lungs, and as she took a deep breath his spicy scent mingled with the fragrant cooking aromas, making her mouth water more than ever.

'Let's go before I change my mind and lose the chivalry act.'

He nuzzled her neck, sending shards of pleasure through her body and she sighed out loud when he pulled away all too quickly.

'You didn't have to go through all this trouble to get me into bed,' she said, gesturing towards the stove-top, the wine and the cosy table for two set in the corner. 'I'm a big girl. I don't need all the trappings.'

His right eyebrow shot up, the small scar adding to his comical surprise. 'Where did that come from?'

She knew.

She'd known the instant she set foot in this room and seen Aidan looking so comfortable, seen the results of his culinary efforts, the effortless way he treated her, a heady mixture of light flirtation with innuendo.

This entire scene was too seductive but not in a sexual way. Seeing him like this, relaxed, contented, casual, scared her more than she'd anticipated.

Sharing a home-cooked meal, having him lavish attention on her with the tempting promise of so much more was terrifying to a girl who craved this more than her next breath, to a girl who normally couldn't think beyond tomorrow, let alone contemplate more than a few dates with the same guy, yet here she was, wishing for for ever with Aidan.

Her stomach churned, her heart flip-flopped and her palms grew sweaty, physiological responses to a psychological problem she was all too aware of.

She might have dated guys who went to loud parties, dance clubs and who wouldn't know coriander from a blade of grass, guys who were like her on the surface: brash, fun, party guys. But each and every time she'd hoped for more, had been on the lookout for the right guy to share a future with.

What if her search had ended? With a guy who had as much chance of sticking around as she did of travelling to Timbuktu with him?

Oh, yeah, she knew exactly why she'd sounded so snippy, but there was no way she'd tell him.

'Sorry, didn't mean to bite your head off. I'm just not used to being spoilt.'

His grip on her hand tightened as he tilted her chin up to stare deep into her eyes.

'Maybe you just need the practice?'

She gulped, captured in the heat radiating from him like warming rays from a welcome winter sun, frightened by how much she wanted to be spoiled by this incredible guy, terrified he'd virtually verbalised her greatest fear: she wanted more from this—thing…fling…whatever they wanted to pass it off as—than he did.

Breaking the hypnotic eye contact by stepping back and swinging their linked hands like a preschooler, she said in an all-too-bright voice, 'Let's take a look around.'

To his credit he didn't push her for answers despite the curiosity clouding his eyes, and tugged her towards the door.

'Lounge room.'

He pointed through a door on the left and she darted a quick glance around, taking in the pine floorboards, Persian rug, tatty cream sofa, crammed bookshelf, open fireplace fanned by a gold peacock guard, a model of an old steamship and a mantelpiece adorned with several rather ugly statues and figurines, immediately struck by how different this was from her place.

Old versus new, antique versus contemporary.

The contrasts served to reinforce the yawning gap between the two of them. Aidan versus Beth.

The thought saddened her more than she'd thought possible for a carefree type of girl who'd bounced into this relationship with a spring in her step and hope in her heart.

'Study's next.'

More antiques, more bookshelves, more old paintings.

'Spare bedroom.'

She barely gave the boring beige room a glance, feeling increasingly nervous as they reached a rather ornate door that had to lead to the master bedroom.

'My room.'

Closing her eyes for an instant, she pictured black satin sheets, ruby-red scatter cushions and mirrored ceilings.

So a girl could fantasise, couldn't she?

'It's not that scary.'

His amused tone alerted her to the fact he'd sprung her daydreaming.

'Says you. For all I know you probably have a fully equipped dungeon in there.'

His eyebrows shot up and she laughed at his horrified expression.

'Relax, I'm kidding. Somehow, I can't see you as the bondage type.'

His eyes darkened with mystery and she swallowed, all too aware of their proximity and the fact there was probably a bed with their names written all over it behind the door.

'I'm not. Though the odd silk scarf or two might come in handy…'

Her breath caught as he slid an arm around her waist and drew her close, slanting a slow burning kiss across her lips, the type of kiss designed to stoke her fire, a kiss that turned her into a quivering mess with the barest flick of his tongue against her lips.

'Have you ever been tied up?' he whispered against the corner of her mouth, his breath sweet from the wine, his piquant blackcurrant scent intoxicating.

Her eyes fluttered shut as he kissed his way towards her ear lobe, and the instant they closed she could see the two of them in vivid detail: naked, her lounging back on satin sheets, Aidan over her, tugging gently on purple silk binding her to a wrought-iron bed…

'You don't have to answer if it makes you uncomfortable.'

He pulled away as she opened her eyes to find him staring at her with concern.

She chuckled, not surprised her laugh had a slight hysterical edge considering she couldn't get the erotic image of the two of them and those sexy silk scarves out of her head.

'You're full of surprises. You're the quiet charmer, I'm supposed to be the wacky, zany one, remember?'

Relief evident in the immediate relaxing of his shoulders, he sent her a quick wink as he threw open the door. 'Haven't you heard the quiet ones are always the worst?'

'I stand duly warned,' she said, exhaling as she stepped into the rather bland room, not sure if she was disappointed or relieved at the lack of satin sheets and silk scarves.

However, her imagination took flight again as he led her into the most gorgeous room in the house, a room at complete odds with the rest.

'The *en suite*,' he said, in the same conversational tone he'd used to announce the rest of the rooms.

'Oh, wow.'

She released his hand and headed straight for the monstrous Jacuzzi mounted in the far corner. 'This is amazing.'

She let her hand drift along the pale green marble, the gold taps, the border edged in exquisite mosaic. 'You must never want to get out of this.'

He propped in the doorway, amused at her drooling over a bath tub.

'Actually, I can't remember ever having a bath.'

'Here, you mean?'

He shook his head, joining her at the tub. 'Ever.'

Aidan saw the confusion in her eyes and felt compelled to explain.

'I showered as soon as I could stand up.'

She snorted. 'You don't know what you're missing. This is one serious bath tub.'

He shrugged and perched on the edge of it. 'Personally, I don't see the attraction.'

'You're kidding.'

With a snap of her fingers, her eyes lit up and she yanked open the vanity cupboard, ducking her head into it and letting out an excited squeal.

Covering his eyes with his hand, he said, 'Don't tell me, you've found evidence my folks aren't the couple of old fuddy-duds I imagine.'

Straightening so fast she almost hit her head on the wash-basin, Beth faced him with a cheeky glint in her eyes and a teasing smile playing about her mouth.

'Don't worry, there aren't any silk scarves if that's what you're worried about.'

He groaned, quickly blotting out that ghastly image. 'You've got a dangerous look in your eyes.'

She advanced towards him, sashaying across the incredibly large bathroom.

'Dangerous, huh? Perhaps you should be afraid.'

She hooked her hands around his neck and pulled him down for a swift, scorching kiss that had all the blood in his head instantly heading south. 'Very afraid.'

He needed little encouragement to prolong the moment, his excitement skyrocketing as she opened her mouth to him again, her tongue slowly meeting his in an erotic, sinuous dance that had him wishing they could stay like this for ever.

For ever?

Oh, no, no way, uh-uh. He didn't do for ever.

The only long-standing commitment he had was to archaeology and he wanted to keep it that way no matter how much he'd like to get to know this crazy woman, every gorgeous, spontaneous inch of her, how much he'd like to spend more than a few months with her.

But he couldn't do it. He'd trodden the relationship road once before and the fallout had sent him high-tailing it back to his digs and he hadn't stopped running since.

Rattled by the startling realisation of how much he wanted more from her than just sex, he backed her against the vanity cabinet, kissing her longer, harder, deeper, hungry kisses that fuelled his fire for her and obliterated the dangerous thoughts of wanting more.

This mind-blowing physical connection they shared he could handle. As for anything more permanent…it just couldn't happen.

'Mmm…'

Her appreciative moan sizzled through his blood and he almost lost it.

However, this wasn't what he wanted from tonight. At least, not till later, after he'd wined her and dined her, chatted and flirted with her, charmed her as she deserved.

Last night at her place had been amazing and he'd replayed it like a XXX movie through his mind all day. But he'd wanted tonight to be about more than sex, about exploring the possibility of the two of them dating for the short time he was in town, and to do that he knew he had to take this slower despite every horny cell in his body telling him otherwise.

Disengaging his mouth with reluctance, he pulled away just enough to trace her lips with his finger, to watch her shining green eyes haze over with passion.

'I need to check the stove before my efforts to impress you go up in smoke.'

She smiled, trying to draw his finger into her mouth but

he was too quick, snatching it away before she undid him completely.

'You've already impressed me and it has nothing to do with your cooking skills.'

Battling a raging libido was hard enough without this incredibly sexy woman staring at him as if she wanted to eat him alive, but he managed to take a few ragged breaths before stepping away.

'How about we eat first and do some serious searching for those silk scarves later?'

Her answering smile, laden with promise, had him thrusting his hands into his pockets—what little room was left—to stop from reaching out and grabbing her.

'Deal. Though you have to promise me one thing.'

'Anything.'

Leaning closer, her breasts brushing against his chest with exquisite torture, she whispered in his ear. 'You give me ten minutes in here later. I think I'll have a surprise you'll really like.'

'Make it five?'

Laughing, she slipped her hand into his and turned towards the door. 'You never cease to amaze me.'

He squeezed her hand in response and tugged her towards the kitchen.

He amazed her, huh? Wait till she saw what he had in mind for after dessert.

'Ready or not, here I come.'

Aidan heard a muffled, 'This isn't hide and seek,' from behind the bathroom door before it creaked open and Beth stuck her head around it.

'You're wearing too many clothes for what I have in mind

in here,' she said, her cheeky grin in contrast to her mock frown as her gaze slid down his body. 'Way too many clothes.'

'Easily rectified.'

He whipped his T-shirt off in record time and flung it on a nearby chair, his fingers snapping the top button of his jeans undone before she reached out and stilled his hand.

'On second thoughts, I'll take care of that.'

Opening the door wider, she stepped aside and gestured him in with a theatrical flourish.

'What the—?'

'I know it's not a guy thing, but you said you'd never taken a bath so I thought now was as good a time as any.'

His jaw dropped as he took in the candles of all shapes and sizes strategically placed around the bathroom to cast an inviting glow, the rose petals floating on the steaming water filling the bath and the topped-up wineglasses within easy reach of the tub.

'I know it's probably not your thing but I thought—'

'It's great. Really.'

He cupped her cheek for a moment, impressed with the effort she'd gone to, blown away by how much thought she'd put into this. 'I take it you got all this stuff from under the vanity?'

'Uh-huh. I'm sure your folks won't mind.'

He didn't care if they did. Right now, all he wanted to do was immerse himself in that tempting body of water, followed by the tempting body of the woman who'd done all this just for him.

'So are you going to step into the bathroom or stay out there all night?'

Smiling, he let her lead him in by the hand, inhaling sharply as a delicious aroma reminiscent of freshly baked sweet rolls slammed into his senses.

'Vanilla and cinnamon bath essence,' she said, reading his

mind as he breathed in several lungfuls of the heady fragrance, wondering if the scent would linger on her soft skin after they bathed together, knowing it would tempt him to taste every inch of her all night long.

Reaching out, he snagged his finger into the top of her flirty skirt and tugged. 'What were you saying a minute ago about me wearing too many clothes?'

'Patience…'

They'd reached the tub and he forced himself to stand perfectly still, his arms loose by his sides as she stepped closer, her fingers toying with his zip while she stared up at him with a naughty glint in her eyes.

'You're killing me,' he muttered as she slid the zip down centimetre by centimetre, the rasp of the metal teeth drowning out his whoosh of air as she completed her task, slid her hands inside the waistband and gently eased the denim off his hips.

'You can't rush a good bath.'

Her sizzling look from beneath lowered lashes would've fried him on the spot if he weren't already near boiling point.

Standing back, she tapped her bottom lip with her finger and stared directly at his crotch. 'Hmm…still too many clothes.'

However, as she reached for his boxers he grabbed her wrist.

'Not so fast. Seeing as this is the first time for me, I'm a little nervous. I think I need my hand held in that tub.'

Her lips curved in a provocative smile. 'Bet that's not all you need held.'

His chuckles died as she shimmied out of her denim mini and jade halter top in a second, leaving her standing less than two feet away from him in a skimpy lace thong the exact striking colour of her top.

'Last one in is a rotten pterodactyl egg,' she said, peeling the lace down her long legs with the panache of someone at total ease with her body before stepping into the bath and sinking below the waterline, ruining his view of the good stuff completely.

Shucking his boxers in record time, he joined her in the bath, his sharp intake of breath having little to do with the hot-water temperature and everything to do with Beth sitting up to make room for him, bringing her nipples to the surface of the water.

'Turn around,' he commanded, eager to feel her flush against him, eager to fill his hands with her.

'Jeez, you're bossy.'

However, she did exactly as she was told, settling her back against his chest, resting her head on his shoulder as they both lay back and let the soothing water overlap them.

'Comfortable?'

'Very,' she murmured, wriggling her butt against his erection to prove it.

'Good. I've heard it's important to relax while having a good soak.'

He cupped her breasts as he spoke, savouring their weight in his palms, lightly pinching the nipples till they stood out in two jutting peaks.

She moaned, her head lolling back further as he slid his hands down her stomach in a long, slow caress till his right hand rested on her mound and he slid a finger between her slick folds.

'Relaxed yet?'

'Getting there.' She gasped, her voice barely audible as her pelvis thrust upwards in reaction to the leisurely exploration of his fingers.

Empowered by her soft mewling sounds, he grazed her clitoris repeatedly, touching her with the lightest of pressure, savouring the thrill of how much he turned her on.

'Aidan…'

Her escalating pants encouraged him to pick up the tempo and in a heartbeat she stiffened and cried out, her head digging into his shoulder as her body thrust upwards out of the water before sinking below the surface on a sigh.

'I'm really getting the hang of this bath caper,' he murmured, slanting a lingering kiss across her mouth, knowing he'd never be able to step into this room again without remembering the electrifying sounds she made as she came.

'This bath was supposed to be all about you.'

She stared at him with wonder in her eyes, large, limpid moss-green pools he could quite happily drown in.

'You don't think I'm enjoying it?'

He gave a little upthrust of his hips, leaving her in little doubt as to exactly how much he was enjoying it.

In response, she sat upright and flipped around, straddling him before he could blink. Bracing her hands on his shoulders, she leaned forward till her nipples brushed his chest, her breath the barest whisper against his cheek. 'I want you.'

With blood pounding through his veins and every cell in his body screaming for release, he forced himself to lean back and intertwine his fingers behind his head, the small part of him wanting to prolong the pleasure vindicated by the hungry glint in her eyes.

Sending her a slow smile designed to tease, he said, 'Then take me. I'm all yours.'

Beth's breath caught as Aidan's erection nudged her entrance and she cursed, darting a frantic glance around in the hope a condom would miraculously appear out of thin air.

'Ah…' He held on to her tight as he surged out of the water. 'I think what you're after is in the bedroom?'

'Actually, it's right here.'

Her hand zeroed in on his erection as she slid down his body to stand dripping on the bathmat. 'But you're right, the bedroom is a great idea considering what I'd like to do with this.'

She gave him a gentle squeeze and he groaned, his tortured expression leaving her in little doubt he couldn't hold out much longer.

'You like?'

Her voice came out a purr and he growled in response, grabbing the nearest towel and enveloping both their bodies, creating an intimate cocoon of hot flesh and barely restrained desire.

'You shouldn't tease a man when he's on the brink,' he murmured, backing her towards the bed when she didn't let up her grip.

'Who said I'm teasing?'

Chuckling, he whipped off the towel as they tumbled onto the king-size bed, its cushiony softness moulding around their heated bodies.

So he didn't have satin sheets? It didn't matter considering the star of her every recent fantasy was propped above her, staring at her as if she were one of his prized artefacts.

'I'm usually a patient man but I've got to tell you right now I'm feeling mighty impatient.'

She sighed, loving the way his eyes lit up when he looked at her, loving the bewitching smile playing about his mouth.

Loving?

Though stunned by the depth of feeling Aidan created within her, she quickly amended her thoughts to liking everything about him.

Loving didn't enter the equation. Not for her. Not when he'd be out of her life quicker than she could say shoe sale.

'We've got all night to take it slow.' She reached up to pull his head down towards her. 'Right now, I think I feel the need for speed.'

'You're amazing,' he whispered against the side of her mouth a second before his lips closed over hers in a heart-stopping kiss that left her panting when he momentarily broke contact to slide the top drawer of the bedside table open, grapple with a condom and sheath himself before picking up where he'd left off.

Her body turned to liquid heat as his hands smoothed over her body, exploring every dip, caressing every curve while kissing her the entire time, deep, hungry, passionate kisses that wiped her mind of all thought bar one: how much she wanted—needed—him inside her this very minute.

As if reading her mind he parted her legs with gentle pressure from his thighs and eased himself into her, inch by exquisite inch, his tongue mimicking exactly what he'd be doing to her for as long as she could hold out.

But she didn't want this time to be slow. She wanted hard and fast and, wrapping her ankles around his butt, she surged upwards, taking him in to the hilt, expanding around him, throbbing with need.

With a loud groan he gave up the last vestige of restraint and started to move, faster, harder, pounding into her as her body strained upwards to meet him thrust for thrust.

Tension coiled, grew, spread upwards and inwards, driving her wild with the mind-numbing pleasure of it all.

She teetered on the verge, hung there for a heart-stopping second before plunging over the other side into orgasmic oblivion, her cries joining his as he skyrocketed to the moon and back right alongside her.

Sinking back into the bed, she welcomed his weight as he lay on top of her for a moment, cuddling her close.

They didn't speak.

They didn't need to, two people in perfect sync.

Oh, yeah, she *liked* a lot of things about Aidan.

As long as she didn't go getting any crazy ideas about that other L word, she could handle liking him just fine.

CHAPTER TEN

BETH had no problems with the morning-after scenario considering they'd already faced that particular situation twenty-four hours earlier.

However, as she padded down the hallway towards the kitchen, following the aromatic trail of sizzling bacon, she knew this was no ordinary morning after.

This was the morning after the night before she'd realised she was in way over her head with this one.

Aidan liked her, as he'd clearly demonstrated with every touch, every intimate smile, every whispered endearment all night.

But did he like her enough to give up life on the digs for a life with her?

'Yeah, Dad, the museum's fine, running like clockwork.'

She paused in the doorway, swallowing the lump in her throat at the sight of him wearing nothing but soft cotton boxers the same dove-grey shade as his eyes, cradling a cordless phone between his ear and shoulder while deftly flipping bacon with the other hand.

His back muscles rippled with every movement of his arm, his long legs sending an instant flush of heat through her as she remembered how they'd felt entwined with hers as he'd slid into her last night…several times…

The sound of his low, harried voice brought her back to the present and she took a step towards the doorway as he spoke.

'I don't know what my plans are at this stage.'

She halted in her tracks, knowing she should make him aware of her presence but holding back, surprised by his exasperated tone.

'Look, I need to get back to South America sooner rather than later so when you know for sure when you're returning, let me know. Staying indefinitely in Melbourne isn't on my agenda.'

Her blood chilled and she gripped the doorjamb for support as her knees threatened to buckle.

He wanted to leave asap.

No matter what they'd shared, how special their connection, she obviously wasn't on his 'agenda'. How could she be when she couldn't hope to compete with his precious bloody job?

'I've got a handle on things down here for now, just make the most of what's left of your recuperating time and I'll talk to you soon.'

She tried to back away from the doorway before he caught sight of her, but she was a fraction late as he turned to grab a plate from the breakfast bar.

'Hey, there you are. Hungry?'

The tenderness in his eyes reached out and beckoned, warm and secure, openly accepting of her.

But she couldn't do this, couldn't pretend.

Faking a smile, she bounced into the room rather than running out the front door with tears streaming down her face. 'Starving. Hope the bacon's crispy.'

'I remember how you liked it from yesterday morning.'

He slid a plate piled high with poached eggs—yokes runny,

just perfect—crispy bacon and hash browns towards her, accompanied by a lingering kiss that had her stiffening.

'What's wrong?'

'Nothing,' she said, far too quickly as she concentrated on dissecting her food with a knife and fork, wishing they didn't have to have this conversation, knowing it was inevitable.

'Beth, look at me.'

Sighing, she placed the cutlery neatly together in the centre of her plate, her appetite vanishing when she raised her gaze to meet his.

'Was it something about last night? Because if it was—'

'This isn't about something you did.'

She dashed a hand across her eyes, shocked by the sudden sting.

She never cried, just as she never set out to fall for a guy who couldn't settle in one place for long.

Well, well, looked like today was a day for firsts.

'Then what? I don't get it.'

He wiped his hands on the tea towel before flinging it on the breakfast bar and stepping around it, coming to an abrupt halt when she shrank away from him, hands held up to ward him off.

'What the hell is going on?'

Her arms dropped to her sides and she shook her head, wishing there were an easy way to say this, all too aware there wasn't.

'This isn't what I want.'

A frown creased his brow, confusion clouding his face. 'What, breakfast?'

'You know what I'm talking about.'

She slid off the bar stool and headed towards the door, needing some distance between them to deliver her walk-out speech.

She had to do this, had to push him away before he broke her heart completely. Not that it wasn't shattered already.

But she needed to keep her job, had to make him believe ending this was her choice for any reason other than the real one: she'd fallen for him and wanted him to stay.

'This little fling we have going on is getting a bit serious.'

Realisation dawned in his eyes as bewilderment gave way to concern. 'But we haven't discussed a relationship.'

'Yet.'

Shaking his head, he braced against the bench-top with his arms, her traitorous body giving a lurch at the way his pecs stood out, the same way they had when he'd been propped over her last night, satisfying her every desire.

'Okay, so you're right. I do want to talk about us, about where this is going, perhaps the possibility of dating while I'm here. In fact, I wanted to do it last night but we got sidetracked.'

His eyes darkened to stormy at the memory of what they'd shared, of how amazing it had been, and she blinked, needing to dispel the intimate spell that had descended on them the minute he'd mentioned last night.

Ignoring the intense regret stabbing her conscience, she squared her shoulders and looked him straight in the eye.

'But that's just it. We're not going anywhere. At least, I'm not.'

The tiny scar above his right eye twitched as realisation widened his pupils.

'So that's what this is about. You think I'm about to leave?'

'Well, aren't you?'

His jaw clenched, his biceps bulging as he gripped the bench-top tighter. 'I don't know how long I'm staying in Melbourne but you're right, it won't be for longer than a few months. But I thought you knew that and were still happy to start things up? Remember, you were the one who pushed this thing between us.'

'So I was.'

Determined to put an end to this before the sting behind her eyes fast turned into a waterfall, she shrugged as if she didn't give a damn.

'Look, I don't want to get all heavy on you, but I think we should stick to work for however long you're staying around.'

He pushed off the bench-top and crossed the kitchen in two seconds flat to take hold of her upper arms, his touch wreaking as much havoc as his words.

'What's changed? I don't get this sudden turnaround.'

Beth couldn't think, couldn't breathe with his hands touching her, even in such an innocuous way. Her skin prickled beneath his hands, wanting more, needing more, and she struggled to break free only to have him hold on tighter.

'You're not walking out of here until we settle this,' he said, his grim expression at odds with the hurt in his eyes.

Swallowing the emotion lodged firmly in her throat, she knew there was only one way to end this. She had to hurt him badly enough for him to let her go.

'Fine. You want to settle this?'

She tilted her chin up, her heart sinking at the flicker of hope that flashed across his face.

'I want something from you I know you can't give so that's why I'm finishing this now, before we get in any deeper.'

'What's that?'

She wriggled in his arms, hating it had come to this, hating the wariness in his eyes but most of all hating herself for being foolish enough in ignoring every inbuilt self-preservation mechanism that could've stopped her from falling for a guy like him.

'Do you really want to know?'

She thrust her chin up, challenging him to push this, to

take it all the way, for the truth would drive him away once and for all.

'Yeah, I do.'

With a toss of her head, she swallowed the huge lump of emotion lodged in her throat and went for broke.

'I want this to be more than a fling. I want you to stick around. And I know that's not going to happen because you can't wait to get out of the museum. I see the way you drag your ass in there every morning. I see your boredom every time you have to resolve small management problems. You're counting down the days till you're back on some site around the world and I don't blame you. You love your job. I just wish your eyes lit up for me the same way they do when you check out some of those old exhibits.'

His hands loosened their grip and she took the opportunity to slip out of his grasp, her heart breaking as guilt warred with realisation in his incredible grey eyes.

Swiping a hand across his eyes as if to obliterate the truth she glimpsed there, he shook his head. 'Archaeology is my life. I can't give it up.'

'You mean you won't give it up.'

She didn't have to add 'for me'. The unsaid words hung in the growing silence, waiting to be acknowledged. As if that would ever happen.

'I tried it once before. It didn't work out.'

A tiny spark of hope flared in Beth's helplessness, encouraging her to give it one last shot.

'You did? Maybe the place you stayed wasn't for you. Maybe—'

'There was a woman. Fenella,' he said, driving another stake through her heart, putting a name to a faceless female she instantly hated for having the power to make him stick around when she obviously didn't. 'She was an art critic. She accompanied me on a dig once and hated it so we lived together in London for a year…'

He trailed off and some strange masochistic urge prompted her to discover the rest. 'And?'

'And I can't do it again.'

'Just like that?'

He dropped his gaze to stare at the floor and she knew in an instant he hadn't told her the whole story.

'Just like that,' he said, a hint of steel underlying his grim pronouncement, the tiny scar near his eyebrow giving an infinitesimal flicker as he frowned.

'Well, I guess we want different things, then, don't we?'

She had no intention of waiting around for his answer, but as she swivelled towards the door he made a strange, almost strangled sound that had her turning back.

'Beth, we could've dated while I'm here. We could've seen where this could lead.'

'Oh, I already know. You're the one who doesn't want to take the risk.'

She forced her feet to move, determined to ignore the pain in her chest, the deep-seated ache that she'd tried her best and her best wasn't good enough, the soul-deep certainty that she'd just lost the best thing to ever to happen to her.

Aidan did what he'd always done when he needed to blow off steam: he dug.

Grabbing an old shovel of his dad's, he headed out into the backyard and stabbed at the soil in the overgrown veggie patch, enjoying the bite of steel in his instep as he pushed down on the shovel, relishing the twinge in his back as he hoisted a monstrous clump of dirt and flung it as far as he could.

He repeated the action over and over, the mindless repetition soothing as always. With every clump he overturned, his tension dissipated till he leaned forward on the shovel and wiped his brow, sweat pouring off him, feeling lighter than he had in months.

He should've been angry.

Hell, he should've been downright fuming after what Beth had said, pushing him for a commitment he couldn't give, taking their relationship from casual to serious in the blink of an eye.

He didn't like being pushed.

Fenella had pushed…and pushed…and pushed, until she'd pushed so hard he'd had no option but to leave.

She'd hated his job, hated the month they'd spent in Greece, hated everything about it: the dust, the heat, the dirt under his fingernails at the end of another glorious day when he'd discovered a priceless piece of history.

She'd pushed him to make a choice, her or his digs, and he'd chosen her out of love. Or so he'd thought. It wasn't till later, much later, that he'd learned the truth and it sickened him to this day.

He couldn't rely on anyone. Not his parents, not the woman he'd made a mistake of falling for back then. He'd learned the hard way his job was the only dependable thing in his life.

Shaking his head, he drove the shovel harder into the dirt, obliterating his memories of a time he'd rather forget, wishing he could forget more recent ones of Beth and the special time they'd spent together just as easily.

Instead, with the sun beating down on him and his muscles aching as they hadn't in ages, all he could think about was how damn good they'd been together.

He hadn't been truly happy since he'd taken over as CEO at the museum and he missed the hands-on digging and discovery work more than he'd thought possible. But for a while having her in his life had made him forget the daily drudgery of acting CEO. She'd brought a welcome spark to his life and now that she'd ended it…

What was he doing sticking around? Going through the motions in another futile attempt at getting his dad's approval? He should know better by now.

Time to move on.

There was nothing left for him here any more.

Swiping his hands down the sides of his jeans, he fished in his pocket for his mobile, almost dropping the thing when it rang.

'Aidan Voss speaking.'

'Aidan, it's Dorothy MacPherson here, from the museum.'

Surprised a volunteer would be calling him, he stabbed the shovel into the dirt and propped a foot on it. 'What can I do for you?'

'I've got a bit of a problem. A transport company in the Northern Territory just rang, requesting up-front payment before they deliver those Aboriginal artefacts from some caves in Kakadu. And there's no one here to authorise it so I don't know what to do. They sounded pretty uptight and said it was urgent so—'

'Have they faxed through an invoice?'

Dorothy paused before clearing her throat with a nervous little cough. 'Um, yeah, but I think the amount is wrong. It's exorbitant.'

See, this was why he couldn't wait to throw in his CEO job. Beth had been right; he faced piddling problems on a daily basis when he'd rather be out in the scorching outback sun, caving in Kakadu himself.

Shutting his eyes, he visualised what it would be like.

He could almost taste the dry dust clogging his throat as it swirled in an ochre cloud as he bounced down a remote track in a four-wheel drive laden with his favourite tools.

He could almost see the mysterious caves, stark against a cloudless blue sky, beckoning a curious archaeologist to discover its hidden treasures.

He could almost feel the rough, craggy walls, the dirt trickling through his fingers, the bluster of hot wind at his back as he moved deeper into the caves.

'Mr Voss?'

His eyes snapped open and as he took in his surroundings, a postcard-size, derelict backyard in suburban Melbourne, disappointment roiled in his gut, thick and heavy.

He gripped the handle of the shovel tightly, tiny splinters of wood driving into the newly formed calluses on his palm, yet he barely registered the sting. It had nothing on the disillusionment exploding through him, the agony of finally waking up and facing the truth.

He couldn't do this any more.

He'd wanted to help Abe out, wanted to show him what sort of a job he could do, but this was crazy. He wasn't happy in the job, he wasn't happy in his personal life now he'd lost Beth.

There was nothing here for him now.

Propping on the shovel, he gripped his mobile to his ear with his other hand. 'Don't worry about the invoice, Dorothy. I'll come in and take care of it. And thanks for contacting me. You did the right thing.'

'Okay, Mr Voss. Bye.'

Snapping his phone shut, he thrust it into his pocket, picked up the shovel and moved over to the empty flower beds. He had a lot of digging to do to ease the driving urge to head to the airport this instant when he couldn't, not till he'd sorted out a replacement at the museum.

At least he now knew what he had to do.

And when it was done, he'd be on the first plane out of here.

Beth trudged into the museum, her feet dragging.

She was *so* over this.

The sooner Lana threw away her crutches and took over the tours, the better. She'd much prefer hiding away in some storage room cataloguing items, away from prying eyes. In the meantime, she would suck it up, act like a big girl and try not to cringe over the stuff she'd said to Aidan.

Try as she might she couldn't get his guarded expression out of her head when she'd told him she wanted more from him than he was willing to give. It had been like watching shutters spring up, effectively locking her out and wiping away what they'd shared in a second.

Then he'd had to go and rub her nose in it by suggesting they date for the short time he was here, expecting her to roll over and play nice before wishing him bon voyage.

She might have been mad enough to fall for him knowing the type of guy he was, but she wasn't completely insane. If she felt like this now, imagine how much harder, deeper, she'd fall if they spent more time together.

Uh-uh, she couldn't do it. Her live-life-for-the-moment motto had taken a severe beating, one from which she'd have a hard time recovering.

She had to go cold turkey to get over him, for, like the finest Brunetti chocolate, one taste had her addicted for life.

'Hey, Beth, wait up.'

Sighing, she fixed her usual 'all's right with the world' smile on her face, something she'd been doing her entire life, and turned to Dorothy.

'Hi, Dot…' The rest of her greeting died on her lips as she

took in the young woman's new shaggy haircut with high-lights falling around her face in soft waves, coloured contact lenses, figure-enhancing bottle-green skirt suit and snappy black patent ballet flats.

'Some transformation, huh?'

'You look fantastic.'

'All thanks to you.' Dorothy did a little pirouette, her confident smile growing by the minute. 'You may not know a lot about the museum but you sure know fashion.'

'You know I'm not really qualified to take tours, don't you?'

Dorothy shrugged. 'All I know is I'm surprised you got the job here when you seem a bit out of the loop.'

She laughed at Dorothy's diplomacy. 'You mean I stink, don't you?'

'Well, when you put it that way...' Dorothy joined in her laughter and she beckoned her over to a secluded spot near the entrance.

'My cousin Lana Walker is the new head curator. She got the job but sprained her ankle badly before she could start. I needed a job so she got me an interview with Abraham Voss and I got it, though he said I also had to fill in as tour guide until Lana's back on her feet.'

Dorothy reached out and squeezed her arm and for the second time in as many hours she blinked back tears. 'Considering your lack of knowledge, you've done great.'

Beth chuckled. 'If you think I'm great, wait till you meet Lana.'

'I can't wait. We should have loads in common.'

Glancing at Dorothy's trendy suit and subtle make-up, Beth doubted it.

'It'll be great for Lana to have a friend when she starts here.

Maybe we can all go for a drink before she starts? There's a new vodka ice bar I've been dying to try.'

Dorothy's eyes lit up. 'Sounds great.'

'Okay, I'll tee it up. Now, must dash. Tours to take, exhibits to be at.'

Dorothy chuckled and waved her off, while Beth turned towards the huge front doors, ready for another history lesson with the boss.

She could do this. After all, it wasn't the first time she'd had to pretend all was right with the world when it wasn't. And while her personal life might have just gone belly up, she didn't need her job to follow suit.

Heading into one of the huge, cavernous storage areas behind the main gallery, she spied Aidan near a glass cabinet where a wooden glider resembling a pigeon was suspended.

She'd already read up on the Saqqara Glider and wanted to give him her spiel and get this history lesson over and done with asap.

Fixing a smile on her face as wooden as the weird birdlike thing behind the glass, she strode towards him, her heels clacking loudly against the marble tiled floor, his head snapping up as she neared.

Her heart stalled as the tantalising, sexy grin she'd grown to love kicked up the corners of his mouth, her knees turning to jelly as the familiar surge of heat whenever he looked at her flooded through her like a hot torrent of desire.

'Right on time.'

He tapped his watch face, instantly transporting her back to the first day she'd walked into the museum and he'd pulled her up for being late. Then, like now, he'd looked as if he wanted to laugh despite his stiff CEO expression and she couldn't help but wish she could turn back time and do things differently.

But would she? Could she have held their overwhelming attraction at bay, ignored the lick of heat whenever they got within two feet of each other? Unlikely, and besides, no use beating herself up over what was done.

She'd wanted to have a little fun. It wasn't his fault she'd been stupid enough to fall for him.

'I've got an extra tour scheduled in half an hour so can we make this quick?'

Her tone was cool, calm and she silently applauded herself on maintaining a professional front when inside she was dissolving with the agony of seeing him and not being able to touch.

His smile faded as he gestured her closer, where she promptly took up position on the opposite side of the cabinet, resting her arms on the top to peer in as if the glider were the most fascinating thing she'd ever seen.

'You read my notes on this?'

'Uh-huh.'

Though for the life of her, she couldn't remember a thing as he stepped around the glass and stood next to her, the fine wool of his designer suit brushing her arm, sending a bolt of heat shooting through her so quick she had to grit her teeth to keep from crying out.

When the awkward silence grew, he sent her an uneasy glance. 'Maybe I'll give you a quick run-down and you can ask questions?'

She nodded, not trusting herself to speak as the faintest waft of blackcurrant drenched her in memories of his bare skin, her nose pressed into the nook of his neck, nuzzling him, drinking in his scent, never getting enough.

'This was found in eighteen ninety-eight in a grave near the Egyptian city of Saqqara and catalogued. It dates to around two hundred BC but didn't attract interest till an archaeologist in nineteen sixty-nine noticed its shape strongly resembled that of a modern glider.'

He cast her another quick glance but she didn't move, her eyes fixed on the artefact, her head still spinning and her body still reacting from his nearness. 'So of course the inevitable questions arose about whether the glider served as a model for real-life larger gliders and whether people of that time were familiar with the flight phenomenon.'

He finished his spiel and looked at her, expecting a response when all she could manage was a lame, 'Uh-huh.'

His gaze roved her face, intense, scrutinising, searching for answers she'd already given him. What more did he want from her?

'Beth, I'm leaving.'

It didn't surprise her, she'd been expecting as much but it didn't lessen the pain clamping her heart and squeezing hard.

'Come with me,' he blurted, his hand shooting out to grab hold of hers as if he expected her to bolt.

Impossible, considering her muscles had seized the moment he'd issued his invitation, the surge of inane joy dwindling to a trickle in an instant as she realised she couldn't do it.

No matter how tempting, she couldn't follow him to the ends of the earth on a whim.

She wanted more out of life now, had taken steps towards achieving her own dreams and she'd exterminated her travel bug around the time her dad had dumped her at Lana's that last time, the month before he'd died: alone, in a grungy motel room, in some remote outback town.

She shook her head, using her hair as a shield, hoping he couldn't read the regret on her face. 'I can't.'

'Can't or won't?'

He'd flung her own words back in her face but it didn't matter. Nothing he said could change her mind.

'We need to give this a go, Beth. See where it could take us—'

'I don't want to follow you around to some far-off dig, waiting for whatever scraps of time you feed me at the end of a day. I want more than that. I want…'

She trailed off, aghast at the wave of emotion swamping her, encouraging her to say things better left unsaid.

'What do you want?'

He tipped her chin up gently, his tenderness unravelling the last of her self-control and she jerked back, unable to stand this a second longer.

'I want you to be happy,' she said, swallowing the truth, tucking her head down and making a break for the door without looking back.

Aidan glanced around his office, not in the least surprised it didn't look any different from when he'd first taken on the job. His few belongings lay scattered across the desk, which proved how he hadn't settled in as much as he'd fooled himself into thinking.

Oh, yeah, this was the best decision for all of them, especially since Beth had made her feelings on accompanying him more than clear.

She was just like Fenella, turning her nose up at life on the digs, not willing to take a chance on him despite what he thought they'd shared.

He was better off without her, better off discovering the truth now before he made another mistake.

As for his dad…well, if Abe didn't agree with his decision to leave now, tough.

His mobile rang on cue and he glanced at the caller, relieved Abe had called back and he could soon put all this behind him.

'Thanks for getting back to me so quickly.'

'Everything all right with the museum? Your message sounded serious.'

Aidan shook his head. Typical Abraham Voss. He could be dying a slow, painful death but the first thing dear old Dad thought about was his precious museum.

'Everything's fine here. I just wanted to let you know I'm leaving. I'll give you two weeks to find a replacement then I'm out of here.'

Abe's harsh intake of breath didn't surprise him, nor did the explosive expletive.

'What brought all this on? The museum needs you.'

He propped against the desk, his heart heavy. Even now, his father couldn't give a fig about why he was really doing this; all he cared about was an inanimate building.

Time to come clean…about everything.

'The only reason I took this job temporarily was to please you. It's pretty much why I became an archaeologist, why I've done a lot of things in my life. It's been the only way to get your attention half the time.'

Another muttered expletive followed by a loaded pause where he could almost hear the wheels in Abe's self-absorbed mind turning.

'This is ludicrous. Your mother and I have always cared about you.'

'Yeah, but caring didn't extend to you being there for my first day at school, or the time I made school captain or the time I was dux at uni. And it sure as hell doesn't extend to you being happy for me now I'm going back to the job I love.'

'Where's all this coming from?'

As expected, his father's audible confusion showed he didn't have a clue.

'Honestly? I should've said this a long time ago. Guess I had hopes you'd change after I helped you out. Not any more.'

To his surprise, he heard distress rather than the anger or defensiveness he'd expected. 'Look, son, I know you like being out on the digs but I thought it would be good to give you a feel for being CEO, see if you liked it before I made any decisions.'

'What sort of decisions?'

Though in that instant, he knew without having to ask: Abe had tried to manipulate him into taking over the top job, which just proved he didn't have a clue what really made him tick.

'Whether I come back or not.'

Running a ragged hand over his face, he took a steadying breath, knowing he had to stay calm to get his point across. If Abe didn't get it now, he never would.

'I was never planning on sticking around, Dad. You wanted me to do exactly what you wanted so you pulled out the sick card, knowing I wouldn't say no. Want to know the stupid part? I thought you needed me for once, that you might actually care enough to reach out. But I was wrong.'

'Well, then.'

Abe exhaled and silence reigned for a few seconds before he cleared his throat as if he had a million frogs stuck in it. 'You're right, I wanted you to take over as CEO permanently, but I knew you wouldn't go for it if I asked, so I thought if you had a little taste of it you'd step up.'

Abe's admission should've eased the bitterness. It didn't. It merely served to reinforce the huge emotional gap between them.

'So you played up your heart problems?'

Abe sighed, sounding wearier than he ever had. 'My blood pressure is under control with medication and I haven't had an angina attack in a while. Yes, I had to take a break on doctor's orders, but not for this long. That was me hoping you'd like the top job enough to stay.'

'You manipulated me. And you know I would never have stuck around more than a few months.'

This time, he spoke without rancour. It was a flat statement, a fact that no amount of ranting or raving or emotion could change. After all these years, Abe didn't get it: how much he loved the hands-on work, how he thrived on the excitement of discovery, how he could never be happy confined behind a desk.

'I was grooming you and this was the only way I could think of to get you to do it.'

No apology, no back down. But then, what did he expect? Selfish people couldn't see what they did was wrong. The end always justified the means.

'I can't change your mind?'

Mentally slapping himself, Aidan said, 'No. And unlike you, I don't only think of myself so like I said I'll give you a few weeks to find a replacement, but after that I'm out of here.'

He could've sworn he heard a choked sound akin to a sob down the line, but that couldn't be right. That would mean his dad cared and he didn't. Not by a long shot.

'You didn't really become an archaeologist just to get my attention, did you?'

It was a good question, something he'd pondered himself over the last twenty-four hours.

'Actually, my career choice wasn't all about you. I guess you and Mum instilled your love of old stuff into me from a young age and hanging around the dig sites just spurred me on. You know, that's the only time you ever paid me real attention, when I found something.'

Another sharp intake of breath let out on a slow hiss. 'I'm sorry, son. I had no idea.'

Just like that, his residual animosity dissolved. Ironic, considering he'd spent a lifetime carrying around this baggage and all it took was a simple apology to lift the weight from his shoulders.

'That's the first time you've ever apologised for anything.'

'I know, and I'm sorry about that too. I'll be flying back once I wrap things up here with the house we've bought. Can we have a man-to-man chat as soon as I get back to Melbourne?'

'I probably won't be around. Maybe next time I'm in town?'

'When will that be?'

'No idea at this stage.'

'Stay in touch, won't you, son?'

'Uh-huh.'

Aidan was reaching for the disconnect button when his dad rushed in. 'Son, your mother and I are proud of you, always have been.'

It was the closest he'd get to a declaration of love and for now it was enough. He knew Abe was a thinker, someone who would ponder this conversation at length before drawing his own conclusions.

'Thanks, bye.'

Thrusting the phone into his jacket pocket, he took a long look around the office before heading for the door.

Time to start winding things up here so he could start living again.

CHAPTER ELEVEN

ONE day to go.

Twenty-four hours between him and freedom.

Aidan watched a few straggling employees head out the door, rolling the kinks out of his neck as he wandered to the locker area to do a last-minute check before closing up.

He'd booked his plane ticket, had done a mini-handover via teleconference to the incoming interim CEO and had tied up all loose ends.

Except one. And he knew just where to find her.

After a quick glance into the locker room to reassure himself they were alone, he strode towards the Glozel Runes, hoping Beth would be there just as he'd asked her.

She'd avoided him for the last fortnight and he hadn't had the heart to follow up. Her work had been faultless and he admired how far she'd come, how hard she'd worked to succeed.

But that was not what this meeting was all about. Oh no, far from it.

He had to convince her to take a chance on him, on them. She had an adventurous streak a mile wide and all he had to do was persuade her to indulge it, and him, by travelling with him. It wouldn't be easy, but he had to give it one last try.

Rounding the corner, his confident steps faltered as he

caught sight of her, looking small, fragile, lonely, sitting on a stone bench near the runes.

He'd chosen this place deliberately, wondering if she'd remember how they'd connected during his first history lesson with her, how she'd shared some of his enthusiasm, albeit reluctantly.

He hadn't forgotten.

He'd merely lost sight of what was staring him right in the face due to his own insccurities. Ironically, it had taken his dad's apology to get him thinking. If a stubborn old coot like Abe could change, maybe it was time he let go of his residual bitterness over the Fenella fiasco and took a chance again?

Comparing Beth to Fenella had been wrong, he knew that now. They were nothing alike. Fenella had been cold, calculating, her warm façade exactly that, a façade. She'd used him, had only wanted him as a way to gain exclusives on the latest finds, an instant boost up the career ladder, the only thing she truly loved.

She hadn't given a toss about him, had been secretly screwing her old boyfriend behind his back the entire time he'd been trying to make a go of their relationship in London, putting his own career on hold for her.

And he'd been stupid enough to compare Beth to her?

The Beth he loved was warm, spontaneous, fun. He'd never met anyone so quirky, so full of life, so ready to put themselves out there despite the risk. She'd done that from the first moment she'd laid her attraction out for him, making it clear in no uncertain terms how she felt about him.

Out of nowhere, it hit him and he stopped dead, backtracking his thoughts to something from a few moments ago... something about the Beth he loved... *loved*?

Hell, it was as simple as that.

All his back-pedalling, all his self-talk that he couldn't rely on anyone, all the baloney he'd been feeding himself about being better off depending on his job rather than people had been a crock.

He loved her and when you loved someone you worked on a compromise, a way to make the relationship thrive.

She didn't want to travel; he wanted her to travel with him. Which meant one of them would have to change their minds or else…

Compromise! The perfect solution came to him in a flash and he wanted to punch the air. But would she believe him after what he'd already said to her? Would she give him another chance?

As she raised her head, her wary gaze locking on his, he knew words wouldn't be enough any more.

It was time for action and, luckily, he knew just what he had to do.

Beth checked the address on the fancy cream cardboard card, looked up at the swank city gallery and back at the card.

The invitation couldn't have come at a better time, considering she'd had the weirdest meeting with Aidan yesterday where he'd praised her work, talked around in circles about job opportunities for enthusiastic employees like her, before mumbling something about a prior engagement and rushing out.

It had been bizarre to say the least, especially when she'd been expecting a proper farewell. Or *a* farewell at least.

She'd heard he was leaving today but hadn't had time to find him, didn't want to find him in reality, unable to face saying goodbye without breaking down, throwing the last of her pride to the wind and begging him to stay.

At least she had this, and as her gaze strayed to the invitation and back to the trendy gallery in front of her she wondered if her head had been so filled with Aidan's impending departure that she'd made a mistake.

This couldn't be the right place.

She'd been invited to check out a possible home for her next collection. Considering it would take at least six months for the lease to come through on her own space, she'd been interested. The weird thing was it looked like this gallery wasn't only thinking of hosting her next collection as everything she'd recently made had already taken pride of place here.

The front windows were filled with twisted metal shrubs, flowers and garden gnomes, her interpretation of the Melbourne Flower and Garden Show, some of her best work.

Cupping her hands against the glass, she pressed her face between them, so shocked she stumbled back.

It wasn't just the front windows housing her work. The whole damn gallery was filled with it, the metal pieces at odds with a heap of old masks and pottery pieces and ceramics. Not to mention her Sydney Opera House taking pride of place on a raised dais in the middle of the room.

'What the...?'

She trailed off as she stepped inside the gallery, her mouth dropping open as Aidan stepped out from behind the glass and chrome counter, looking more relaxed than she'd ever seen him.

'What are you doing here?'

He didn't respond immediately, his charismatic smile sending her belly into a free fall she had no hope of recovering from.

It had always been like this, from the first minute she'd met him, and despite everything that had happened between them it looked as if her reaction to the sexy archaeologist hadn't waned at all.

'Well? What's this all about?'

He shrugged, his shoulders looking impossibly broad in

black cashmere as he came around from behind the counter to stand in front of her.

'This is our place.'

'Our place?'

She shook her head, feeling as if she'd stepped into a time warp or some weird alternative universe where everyone knew what was going on but her.

'I want a place to showcase our work so I've leased this space, bought the unsold pieces from your last collection, trumped the top bidder for the fund-raiser piece and added some of my own stuff. I'm confident we can keep the place stocked with your work and my new finds.'

'Ri-i-ight…' She did a slow three-sixty in the middle of the gallery, her confusion intensifying. 'You know none of this makes any sense? I can understand you leasing this place for your stuff, but what's it got to do with me? And why have you spent a small fortune on my work?'

He reached out and tipped her chin up, his smile patient. 'Because it's worth it. You're worth it.'

Brushing away his hand—she couldn't think with the havoc his touch wrought on her body—she took a step back before she swayed towards him. 'Obviously not worth enough. I hear you're still leaving.'

'You're wrong. I can't put a price on what you're worth.'

She took another step back at the intent in his eyes: way too confident, way too intense, way too focussed—on her.

'So what are you trying to say? That you're sticking around here to run this place?'

Her heart leaped at the thought before his serious expression plummeted it back down to earth and trampled all over it. Of course he wasn't sticking around. Then what was this gallery in aid of?

'You know I can't stay in Melbourne permanently.'

'Wow, tell me something I don't know.' Her sarcasm fell on deaf ears as the sexy smile she'd grown to love dazzled her as usual.

'I have to get back to doing what I love, but I thought it would be nice to have a base here, somewhere I could come back to for a few months out of the year?'

Just like that, his motives for leasing this place became crystal-clear.

He expected her to be waiting around for him whenever he decided to drop into town, all dewy-eyed and super-excited the hotshot archaeologist deigned to pay her some attention for part of a year.

Damn him, he was just like her father and she couldn't stand another minute of this.

She clenched her hands to stop from reaching out, grabbing his shirt and shaking him silly. How could he think so little of her? How could he cheapen what they'd shared?

Thrusting her chin up, she tossed her hair over her shoulder in an 'I don't give a damn' gesture. But she did. And, worse, a small, deluded part of her still hoped that by some miracle he'd ditch his travel plans for her.

'So what do you want me to say? I'm happy for you?'

Stepping into her personal space, he ran a hand lightly up her arm. 'I want you to ask me what this has to do with you.'

'No.'

She bit down on her bottom lip to keep from crying out as his hand slipped into hers, his thumb slowly caressing her palm in small circles.

'Fine, I'll tell you anyway. You said you wouldn't travel? Well, this is a compromise.'

'You think by mingling the stuff we do for a living I'll change my mind?'

She shook her head, hating how impressed she was by the effort he'd gone to, how tempted she was to renege on her previous stance and follow him to the ends of the earth to be with him.

But she couldn't.

She didn't want a nomadic life again; she didn't want the scraps of affection he'd throw her way at the end of a busy day. She wanted a man who loved her to put her needs first, to put her first, and that man wasn't Aidan. He'd already made it clear his first love was archaeology and how could she compete with that?

'This place doesn't change a thing.'

His cool expression faltered for the first time since she'd arrived, the scar above his right eye twitching ever so slightly.

'You're scared.'

'Of what?'

She forced a laugh and wrenched her hand out of his, needing space before she leaned into him and wiped the worried look off his face with a kiss she so desperately wanted to deliver.

'Of seeing whether this could work. Of how damn good we could be together if we both try.'

Every tiny arrow of truth he shot at her found its mark, embedding in her heart and rendering her speechless with the pain of it.

Balling her hands, she tugged her bag in front of her, knowing it would prove useless as a shield if he touched her again.

'This is irrelevant. You're going away and I'm not the sit-at-home-and-knit type while I wait for you to drop in whenever you're in the neighbourhood.'

'Ah…but you wouldn't have to wait at home for me.'

Thrusting a hand into his back pocket, he handed her a slimline black folder.

'Here. This should clear up a few more of your preconceptions.'

Flipping open the folder, she stared at the airline ticket, destination Rio de Janeiro, more confused than ever when she spied her name in the 'passenger' box.

Her gaze flew to his, annoyed by his calm demeanour, hating the crazy, out-of-control feeling swamping her. 'I've already said no to travel with you. What's this supposed to mean?'

'We're alike, you and me. We're adventurers. We like to live each day as it comes. We're spontaneous. I understand you don't want to spend your life on the road, you've already been there, done that, but this would be different. We'd be together. We could see how things go.'

Her stunned gaze dropped to the ticket in her hand, the fine print blurring as she blinked back tears of frustration.

See how things go… She didn't need to see, she knew how things would go. She'd soon tire of the travel, she'd start taking it out on him, blaming him for not putting her needs first and they'd end up hating each other.

If her heart was breaking now, it would be nothing on the pain of spending more time with him, falling deeper only to find she'd lose him in the end.

She couldn't do that; she wouldn't.

'Here's the proof of how much I want this to work, Beth. I want you to travel with me to South America. I want you to give us a chance. I want a relationship with you. Quite simply, I want it all.'

Before she could move he captured her face between his hands and crushed his mouth to hers, the kiss a startling combination of heat, passion and desperation, a soul-drugging kiss designed to bewitch, bother and bewilder.

And she was definitely all three, her mind shutting down the instant he deepened the kiss, his tongue eagerly searching out hers, his lips softening, his hands leaving her face to slide down her torso and cup her butt, drawing her firmly against him.

She knew this would have to stop, would have to be the last kiss they ever shared, so she gave herself into the bliss of the moment, taking as well as giving, savouring every sigh, every caress, imprinting it on her brain to be resurrected at will.

'Say yes,' he whispered, his thumbs brushing the corners of her mouth, his incredible slate eyes beseeching her to agree.

For one heart-rending, hope-filled moment, Beth wanted to throw caution to the wind and say yes.

She wanted to fling every reservation she had out the window and go for it.

But she couldn't, for while her heart was screaming 'yes, yes, yes' her head resurrected memories of being dragged from town to town, putting up with the empty, hollow life for love of a man.

She'd loved her dad and in his own selfish way he'd loved her too, but her needs had always come last and she wouldn't let history repeat itself.

'I can't.'

She turned away, dashing a hand across her eyes, simultaneously dashing any faint hope for both of them.

Aidan didn't reach out to her again.

He didn't move, didn't speak, and she finally raised her eyes to meet his, his pain quickly masked by a puzzling perceptiveness.

'I'm sorry. You summed it up when you said you wanted it all. And this way, you'd have it.'

She lifted her hands in a helpless gesture before letting them fall uselessly to her sides, trying not to take great gulps of air to fill her oxygen-deprived lungs, to ease their seizing, to ease the pain squeezing her heart in a vice.

'We could both have it all.'

He reached out to her, but she shook her head and turned away, unable to look at him a moment longer.

'My idea of having it all is staying in one place long enough to build a home, a family. I want my kids to live in a rambling old house with an attic housing their mother's crazy metal sculptures, a tyre on a rope in the back yard and a sprawling oak tree where we could have spur-of-the-moment teddy-bear picnics. I want them to stay in the one grade long enough to make friends. I want them to know that when they ride their bikes home from school there won't be a 'for rent' sign tacked on the front gate. That's what I want.'

Her breaths came in short, sharp pants as her mini-rant wound down and she swallowed the sob that bubbled up in the back of her throat.

How she'd craved those things herself, would've given anything to have them. While her dad might not have cared enough about her to grant her wishes, she'd do her utmost to ensure her kids never had to go through what she did.

'That's great, Beth, but there's a lot to say for kids travelling the world, being steeped in new cultures, learning through hands-on life experience rather than a textbook.'

She stiffened as he came up behind her and rested both hands on her shoulders. 'I should know—I was one of those kids. I loved visiting new places as a kid. I loved the freedom, the buzz. It was one long adventure for a kid and it was great.'

Shaking her head, she blocked out the tiny voice that partially agreed with him, the voice that pointed her to reassess her own memories of her childhood and recognise it hadn't been all bad.

It *had* been fun discovering new towns.

It *had* been exciting exploring every nook and cranny of the places they'd rented.

And there was no denying she'd gained her adventurous spirit from those times.

But overshadowing the good memories were the bad: the teasing for the new kid on the block, the lack of friends, the constant daily fear that today would be another day she'd come home to find her meagre belongings packed and shoved into the back of her dad's beat-up van.

She couldn't subject her kids to a life of uncertainty; it wouldn't be fair.

With agonising regret, she dropped her head to stare at her shoes, finding little comfort in the sparkly ruby crystals winking up at her from her favourite Mollini flip-flops.

Steadying her weakening resolve, she knew she had to end this right now.

'We want different things, Aidan. I'm sorry.'

He didn't move, didn't speak, and she willed herself to move, to shrug his hands off and take that first, final, inevitable step away from him.

Instead, she stood there, her back absorbing his radiant heat, relishing the weight of his hands on her shoulders, wishing he'd never let go.

After what seemed like an eternity, he bent to murmur in her ear, 'Life's an adventure, sweetheart, and I think we both want the *same* thing. The ticket is yours. I leave tomorrow. I'll wait for you at the gate.'

'Please don't.'

Her whispered plea sounded pathetic in the loaded silence

and with a gentle squeeze of her shoulders and a tender, lingering kiss on the nape of her neck he walked away.

Leaving her more confused than she'd ever been in her entire life.

Beth stumbled from the gallery in such a daze it took her a full half-hour and a tram-ride to Lana's house before she realised she still had the plane ticket clutched in her hand.

She'd thrust it into her jacket pocket where it now burned a hole, a reminder of what she could have if she took a chance.

How ironic, that risk was her middle name yet when it came to taking the ultimate gamble—with her heart—she was as yellow-bellied as a low-down snake.

'You better come in before you wear out my footpath.'

Lana held open her front door and it took Beth a full five seconds to absorb what was different about her cousin.

'Hey, no crutches!'

Lana did a little twirl, ending in a stumble. 'Not bad, huh? Almost as good as new.'

'That's great.'

'I thought you'd be happier?' A tiny worry line creased Lana's brow and Beth shook her head, knowing she shouldn't have come here, having no one else to turn to.

'This isn't about you.' Beth gnawed on her bottom lip. 'It's about me being a stubborn mule.'

Lana chuckled. 'Is that all? For a moment I thought it was serious.'

'It is serious, if you consider me being offered the world by an amazing guy and turning it down serious.'

The worry line reappeared as Lana opened the door wider. 'You better come in. This calls for chocolate.'

'It'll take ten blocks to even begin to cure me.'

'You've been bitten, I see.'

Lana rummaged through her pantry before plonking a family-size block of nougat chocolate on the table and flicking the kettle on.

'Bitten?'

Beth broke off an entire row of mouth-watering chocolate and stuffed the six small blocks into her mouth at once, hoping the sugar and cocoa fix would ease her pain. It didn't.

Lana propped against a bench and grinned. 'By the love bug.'

'Ha, ha, you're a real riot.' She reached for the chocolate again before pushing it away with a groan. 'What am I doing? Stuffing myself till I'm sick isn't going to solve anything.'

'But the endorphins will make you feel better.'

She could think of a much better way to get her endorphins going and it had nothing to do with eating chocolate and everything to do with getting naked with the one guy who had rocked her world.

'So you fell in love with the boss? Nice.'

'He's not our boss any more.'

Lana straightened so fast she knocked a spatula off the bench and it clattered to the floor. 'What?'

'He's going back to archaeology.'

'But what about the museum?'

'I'm sure it's still there. After all, it ran perfectly well before he arrived on the scene, right?'

'Right.' Lana nodded, her eyes round orbs behind her glasses. 'Of course, I'm being silly. A guy with Aidan Voss's reputation wouldn't leave the museum in the lurch.'

Lana paused, before snapping her fingers. 'Oh-h-h…now I get it. That's why you're upset? Because he's leaving?'

Beth shook her head. 'He asked me to go with him.'

'What?'

Lana's screech had Beth reaching for the chocolate again. 'Oh, my goodness, that's the most romantic thing I've ever heard.'

'Hold on to your feather boa, Barbara Cartland. I turned him down.'

'You what? But why?'

'Because he wants me to leave everything behind here and travel with him.'

Lana frowned. 'And?'

'I can't do it. You know why.'

The kettle whistled at that moment and Lana busied herself making two hot chocolates complete with marshmallows before taking a seat at the dining table and pushing a steaming mug across to Beth.

'Do you remember what you said the night I got the job?'

Beth took a sip of the hot chocolate and sighed, savouring the slide of rich chocolate across her tastebuds.

'Honestly, cuz? I don't have much recollection of what I said that night. As I recall, I was pretty wasted, celebrating *your* dream job.'

Leaning forward and fixing her with the 'listen up' glare she'd had down pat since childhood, Lana said, 'You said you wanted a family of your own. Hubby, kids, the works, but you didn't want to give up your independence to do it. You still wanted to have fun, be spontaneous, and wished you could meet a guy with a similar outlook.'

'I said that?'

She hid behind her mug, silently vowing to stay clear of celebratory cocktails no matter what the occasion.

'There's more. You offloaded about your dad and how you hated travelling around with him, how the only time you ever felt settled was those times you visited me.'

'Well, like you didn't know that already. You were there the whole time—you saw it.'

'I also saw how you lit up when he came back to get you after those visits, how you talked non-stop about the adventures you'd had together and the places you'd been, how you'd be packed and ready to go each and every time.'

Lana sat back and plucked at the edge of the tablecloth, sending Beth concerned glances from behind her glasses.

'I think you wanted what you couldn't have, Beth. All your dad ever wanted was to find happiness after he lost your mum and having you with him made him happy. Couldn't you see that?'

'Of course I could,' she snapped, instantly regretting her outburst when Lana flinched. 'Look, I'm sorry. I know you're just trying to help but my dad—'

'Was there for you, wanted you with him when he could've just as easily palmed you off onto us full time. You are who you are because of him, don't you see?'

'No! It's because of him I can't do this!'

Her last words came out a sob and she swiped a hand over her eyes, holding up her other hand to stop Lana from hugging her.

'He spent years and years wandering aimlessly, dragging me with him, in search of goodness knows what. He knew what I wanted, how much I wanted a home, but he put his needs first and I won't let any man put his needs above mine ever again. It's masochistic.'

Lana rested her hand gently on Beth's shoulder. 'Aren't you the one who's always raving on about living life to the fullest, about making the most of every minute? Well, from where I'm standing, looks to me like you're not living by your own motto. How is shutting yourself off from this

amazing opportunity with a guy you really like living life
to the full?'

'I don't like him, that's the problem.'

'Huh?'

'I love him.'

Her admission came out on a sigh, a heartfelt, soul-deep
admission ripped from within.

She'd been a goner from the first time he'd called her
Fancy Feet, but she'd done her best to ignore the truth or
sugar-coat it in terms like fling and liking him. Whichever way
she looked at it, she was in love with Aidan, every impressive, delicious inch of him.

'So let me get this straight. You love him but don't want to
have the time of your life because he asked you to travel with
him?'

I love him.

The three little words echoed through her mind, her heart,
reaching down to her soul and making her ache with the joy
of it. She loved a charming, warm, sexy guy who was offering
her the world…and she'd said no.

Was she nuts?

Maybe she should take a chance? Her heart clenched at the
thought, a lifetime of being cautious shadowing her emotions,
whispering, It's not worth the pain.

But she was in pain now, a constant deep-seated ache she
couldn't shake no matter how much she tried to convince
herself she'd made the right decision.

She loved him.

It all came back to that.

Did she have the guts to confront her fear, embrace it and
take a chance on a once-in-a-lifetime kind of love?

'Yes, I love him and I'm scared to admit it for fear of playing second fiddle to his needs. Go figure?'

'But you're the ultimate risk-taker. I just don't want to see you cheated out of happiness when this could be the best risk you ever take.'

'Risk *is* my middle name,' Beth muttered, a small flame of hope quickly fanned by excitement and anticipation and a wealth of possibilities growing to a raging inferno of optimism in a second.

She could do this.

Why not take the risk of a lifetime on a guy that was so-o-o worth it? A guy who'd tried to compromise, a guy who made her feel safe and secure, something that came from being with him and not in one place.

Security didn't come from an inanimate building, it came from being with the man she loved, and as long as they were together she'd always feel safe.

'Does that mean—?'

'It means you're the best cousin in the whole world.' She leaped from her chair and flung herself at Lana, squeezing her in a bear hug till they both laughed. 'Now, if you don't mind, I have some serious packing to do.'

She left Lana shaking her head, a serene smile on her face, and raced out the door, the plane ticket making comforting crinkling noises in her back pocket with every step.

She might have doubt demons dogging her, but it was time to face her fears.

She just hoped it wasn't too late.

CHAPTER TWELVE

AIDAN scanned the dwindling crowd at the gate, his heart sinking with every passing minute.

Beth hadn't come.

He'd given her an option to have the best of both their worlds, he'd given her his heart and she hadn't wanted any of it.

Hoisting his duffel onto his shoulder, he handed over his boarding pass, scrounging up a polite smile for the attractive hostess who looked as if she mightn't be averse to giving him a farewell kiss in lieu of Beth's absence.

Beth...

Damn it, was he ever going to get over her?

She'd blown into his world like a dervish, a bright, sparkly, effervescent breath of fresh air that made him feel as if he could take on Mount Everest and conquer it with one hand tied behind his back.

She'd made him feel alive, had filled all those tiny holes in his heart he'd barely acknowledged existed.

He didn't need to do anything to grab her attention, she'd given it unreservedly from the moment she'd bowled up to him with those bizarre feathery black shoes.

He loved her.

And it was over.

Every step down the long causeway was a step further away from her, a step towards closure.

He had his job.

He had his old life back.

And it wasn't enough.

Clamping his jaw tight, he nodded at the hostess at the door, ready to take his seat, plug his ears with headphones and drown out the world.

'Excuse me, sir.'

'Yes?'

What now? The plane had engine trouble? His seat was next to a faulty exit door?

'You've been upgraded to first class. If you'll follow me?'

Managing a wry smile at the twist of good luck after so much bad, he turned left and followed the hostess.

'You're seated in 1A. Enjoy your flight.'

'Thank you…'

His jaw dropped as he registered the wide, leather seat next to him was taken—by the last person he'd expected to see.

'Hey there, Professor. Thought you might like some company on a long-haul flight?'

He flopped into the chair, the duffel sliding off his shoulder and plopping at his feet, at a loss for words as he stared at Beth and wondered if she was a by-product of his wishful thinking.

'This is a surprise,' he finally managed, trying not to stare at her funky striped midriff top showing a tantalising glimpse of cleavage and her bright orange flip skirt ending halfway up her smooth thighs.

Those legs…he'd caressed those legs, kissed them, nibbled them, had them hold him in a vice-like grip, had explored every gorgeous inch of them, and he clenched his hands into fists to stop from reaching out and touching her.

'Yeah, well, I came into a lot of money because some crazy, spontaneous, sexy guy bought all the unsold pieces from my last collection and, seeing as I love to do spur-of-the-moment things, I thought I'd blow a major part of my earnings on a first-class upgrade.'

While her mouth curved into its signature sassy smile, uncertainty flickered in her beautiful green eyes.

Despite her bravado in showing up here like this, the woman he loved was nervous. And she had no need to be. She'd taken this gigantic step in following him and he would never let her down.

'I'm glad you're here.'

Her mouth drooped in disappointment and he cursed, grabbing her hand to anchor himself, his thoughts.

'That didn't come out right. Guess I'm so blown away by you being here I can't think straight, let alone put into words what I'm feeling.'

'Then let me.'

She leaned forward and brushed her lips over his, a gentle, sensual kiss that had heat searing his body from his head to his feet and concentrating on the bits in between.

He needed little encouragement to deepen the kiss and as she grabbed at the front of his shirt, bunching it in her fists and dragging him closer, he lost it, crushing her close, tasting her, caressing her, unable to get enough. Never enough.

The sound of a discreet little cough penetrated his lust-hazed mind and he pulled back reluctantly, raising his gaze to meet the hostess's rather bland one, as if she'd seen it all before.

'Champagne?'

Beth laughed, a joyous sound that made his heart sing, not in the least embarrassed as she reached across him. 'Love one, thanks. Professor?'

'Thank you,' he said, noting the spark of interest in the hostess's eyes as she looked him over, probably wondering if he was really a professor whisking a student off for a little lovin' South American style.

'She thinks we're having an affair.' Beth smirked at him from behind her flute, her green eyes sparkling.

'Well, she's mistaken. We're in a relationship.'

'Yes, we are.'

She held his gaze and he sighed in relief, eternally grateful she'd changed her mind.

As if sensing the direction of his thoughts, she said, 'I owe you an explanation.'

'You don't owe me anything.'

He brushed the back of his hand against her cheek, loving it when she rested against him for a moment before straightening.

'Actually, I do. You've been incredibly patient and I've behaved like a brat. I want us to start afresh and to do that you have to know what you're getting into with me.'

'Okay, shoot.'

Draining the rest of her champagne, she placed the flute on the console rest before laying a reassuring hand on his leg.

'I've never been involved in a relationship before.'

'Ever?'

She shook her head, blonde hair cascading around her shoulders like the finest gold.

'It's all a bit Freudian, actually. My parents had the perfect relationship. You know, the real soul-mate thing, and as a kid I wanted something exactly like it but that all changed when Mum died.'

'Why?'

He laid his hand on top of hers, hoping his soothing touch was all the incentive she needed to keep going no matter how painful.

'She was the love of my dad's life. He shut down emotionally when he lost her, then tried to make up for it by beginning a never-ending quest for something else to fill the void. I just happened to be along for the ride. Having me around was never enough.'

'I'm sorry.'

Beth raised her gaze from where she'd been focussed on their joined hands, admiring the strength in Aidan's and how perfectly hers fitted in it.

'I am too. Everything I've done since he died, how I've lived my life, the choices I've made, were all shaped by him. Or not wanting to be like him, to be precise.'

'But you're nothing like your dad if he shut down. You're bright and bubbly and live life on full throttle.'

'Yeah, but somehow the "life's short, play hard" motto didn't work when I met you.'

'Why?'

He frowned and she reached up to smooth it away. 'Because I was terrified of how you made me feel. You're the guy I've dreamed of meeting my entire life, the guy I want to stick around with for the long haul. The guy who makes me dream of that house with the attic and the oak tree and the old tyre hanging from it. The guy who loves adventure as much as I do but who I was scared of losing because of it.'

'That's not going to happen.'

He captured her hand as it left his brow and drew it towards his mouth where he placed a slow, lingering kiss on her palm.

'You're not going to lose me.'

'I meant by you travelling around, putting your needs ahead of mine—'

'That's not going to happen. We're a team, a partnership. The gallery is just the start.'

He nibbled his way up towards her wrist, his lips hot against her throbbing pulse as he nibbled the skin over it.

'I better not lose you.' She smiled as he nipped at her wrist. 'You know, I hear archaeology is a dangerous profession. You could fall down one of those giant big holes you dig while searching for some relic. You could get crushed by an ancient ruin tumbling on your head. You could—'

'Fall even harder than I already have,' he murmured, silencing her with the type of kiss she could only dream about.

'Fall?'

'In love with you.'

Her breath caught as the warmth of his smile reflected in his eyes, bathing her in the reassurance she so badly needed.

'I love you too.'

She cupped his face in her hands, holding him, beseeching him to understand what it meant for her to verbalise her feelings out loud. 'And if you're willing to take a risk on an extroverted, fun-loving metal sculptor with a shoe fetish, I'm all yours.'

'No risk.'

He captured her hands and slowly slid them down his torso till they rested over his heart, the steady beat another reminder of how good this guy was for her.

He would show her the world and a million different ways to enjoy it; she would build a home for them when they tired of travelling.

He'd feed her thirst for adventure, she'd feed his soul with fabulous reasons to come home.

Yin and Yang.

Two perfect halves making a whole.

'No risk at all. We're a sure thing.'

'Too right,' she said, sliding her hands out from under his

to delve into her bag. 'By the way, I got you a little going-away present.'

Biting on the inside of her cheek to stop from laughing, she handed him the small black foil-wrapped parcel, which he turned over several times, prodded and shook before slowly pulling on the gold ribbon binding it.

'Hurry it up. We'll be in Rio by the time you open it.'

'Haven't you heard the old saying good things come to those who wait…?'

The rest of what he'd been about to say died on his lips as the wrapping fell open to reveal a matching pair of exquisite amethyst silk scarves, which he picked up and slid through his fingers, the slow, sensuous movement causing heat to flow through her body as he stared at her with desire.

'Does this mean you want to tie me up?'

'For ever,' she murmured, tugging on the scarves, bringing him close enough to kiss.

'Sounds like a plan.'

And as the plane taxied down the runway, they made a few more.

'Six months on the road at digs, six months in Melbourne for you to sculpt?'

'Deal.'

'We keep the gallery and use it to showcase our talents?'

'Deal.'

'We give this relationship a trial before doing the "till death do us part" thing?'

'No deal.'

Hating the momentary panic flaring on his face, she said, 'Who needs a trial? Some smart guy once said we're both adventurers. So how about it? You in this for the long haul?'

'With you by my side I'm up for anything.'

'Really?'

She sent a pointed glance at his groin, raising an eyebrow.

'You're killing me, Fancy Feet.'

'Not yet, but it's a long flight, Professor,' she said, draping a blanket over his lap and sliding her hand up his thigh.

He clamped a hand over hers, laughing when she struggled and the blanket became a tug of war.

'I can get used to this.' He angled in for a swift kiss, which disarmed her completely. 'Travelling together, having *fun* together…'

'I'm all for fun.' She tugged the blanket back over both of them and snuggled into him, more content than she'd ever been. 'And I'm also all yours.'

'Right back at you.'

And as Aidan hugged her close, the plane soared skywards and Beth hummed 'Love is in the Air' under her breath she knew without a shadow of a doubt that some risks were worth taking.

All the way.

* * * * *

Carefully, Wren released her weight from his, but considered how much better the day might be spent there. Bad morning to go, longer days to stay...

...during turn and drink, her mouth close to his... She clearly had because she had... sipped...

...she gave him... coffee.

After taking a sip, he smiled and said, "Good morning, Colton," hope the floor wasn't too hard for you."

The huskiness of the flow didn't been too insolent. She stroked her head "were you kidding? I sleep like a baby," he added in... wasn't going back...

to my usual... experiences."

...If he wanted to get technical, yeah, "I hurt, for the tenor, it made sleeping on the floor almost bearable." As had the warmth of his warmed body. She thought, then quickly

"Is that for me?" Trey asked.

Cardin Worth cocked her head to the side and considered how much better the day already seemed. "Good morning to you, too."

When she didn't hold out the second cup of coffee for him to take, he came closer. She sipped from her heavy white mug, hiding her grin and her giddy rush of nerves behind it.

But when he stopped in front of her, she made the mistake of lowering her gaze from his face to the exposed strip of his chest. It was either give him his cup of coffee or bury her nose against him and breathe in. She remembered so clearly how he smelled. How he tasted.

She gave him his coffee.

After taking a quick gulp, he smiled and said, "Good morning, Cardin. I hope the floor wasn't too hard for you."

The hardness of the floor hadn't been the problem. She shook her head. "Are you kidding? I slept like a baby, swaddled in my sleeping bag."

"In my sleeping bag, you mean."

If he wanted to get technical, yeah. "Thanks for the loaner. It made sleeping on the floor almost bearable." As had the warmth of his spooned body, she thought, then quickly changed the subject. "I saw you have a loaf of bread and some eggs. Would you like me to cook breakfast?"

He lowered his coffee mug slowly, his gaze as warm as the sun on her shoulders, as the ceramic heating her hands. "I didn't bring you out here to wait on me."

"You didn't bring me out here at all. I volunteered to come."

"To help me get ready for the race. Not to serve me."

"It's just breakfast, Trey. And coffee." Even if last night it had been more. Even if the way he was looking at her made her want to climb back into that sleeping bag. "I work much better when my stomach's not growling. I thought it might be the same for you."

"It is, but I'll cook. You made the coffee."

"That's because I can't work at all without caffeine."

"If I'd known that, I would've put on a pot as soon I got up."

"What time *did* you get up?" Judging by the sun's position, she swore it couldn't be any later than seven now. And, yeah, they'd agreed to start working at six.

"Maybe four?" he guessed, giving her a lazy smile.

"But it was almost two…" She let the sentence dangle, finishing the thought privately. She was quite sure he knew exactly what time they'd finally fallen asleep after he'd made love to her.

The question facing her now was where did this relationship—if you could even call it *that*—go from here?

* * * * *

*Cardin and Trey are about to find out that
great sex is only the beginning....
Don't miss the fireworks!
Get ready for
A LONG HARD RIDE
by Alison Kent
Available March 2009,
wherever Blaze books are sold.*

HARLEQUIN *Presents*

ONE NIGHT BABY

When passion leads to pregnancy!

PLEASURE, PREGNANCY AND A PROPOSITION
by Heidi Rice

With tall, sexy, gorgeous men like these,
it's easy to get carried away with
the passion of the moment—and end up
unexpectedly, accidentally, shockingly

PREGNANT!

Book #2809

Available March 2009

Don't miss any books in this exciting new
miniseries from Harlequin Presents!

HARLEQUIN *Presents*

International Billionaires

*Life is a game of power and pleasure.
And these men play to win!*

AT THE ARGENTINIAN BILLIONAIRE'S BIDDING
by *India Grey*

Billionaire Alejandro D'Arienzo desires revenge
on Tamsin—the heiress who wrecked his past.
Tamsin is shocked when Alejandro threatens her
business with his ultimatum: *her name in tatters
or her body in his bed...*
Book #2806

Available March 2009

Eight volumes in all to collect!

HARLEQUIN *Presents*

*Introducing an exciting debut
from Harlequin Presents!*

Indulge yourself with this intense story
of passion, blackmail and seduction.

VALENTI'S
ONE-MONTH MISTRESS
by *Sabrina Philips*

Faye fell for the sensual Dante Valenti—but he
took her virginity and left her heartbroken. She
swore *never again!* But he wants her back,
and what Dante wants, Dante takes....

Book #2808

Available March 2009

Look out for more titles from Sabrina Philips
coming soon to Harlequin Presents!

THE BILLIONAIRE'S CONVENIENT WIFE

Forced to the altar for a marriage of convenience!

He's superrich, broodingly handsome and
needs a bride in name only....

She's innocent yet defiant, and she's about to be
promoted from mistress to convenient wife!

Look for all of our exciting books in March:

The Italian's Ruthless
Marriage Bargain #45
by KIM LAWRENCE

The Billionaire's
Blackmail Bargain #46
by MARGARET MAYO

The Billionaire's
Marriage Mission #47
by HELEN BROOKS

Jonas Berkeley's
Defiant Wife #48
by AMANDA BROWNING

www.eHarlequin.com

REQUEST YOUR
FREE BOOKS!

2 FREE NOVELS
PLUS 2
FREE GIFTS!

PASSION
GUARANTEED
SEDUCTION

YES! Please send me 2 FREE Harlequin Presents® novels and my 2 FREE gifts (gifts are worth about $10). After receiving them, if I don't wish to receive any more books, I can return the shipping statement marked "cancel". If I don't cancel, I will receive 6 brand-new novels every month and be billed just $4.05 per book in the U.S. or $4.74 per book in Canada, plus 25¢ shipping and handling per book and applicable taxes, if any*. That's a savings of close to 15% off the cover price! I understand that accepting the 2 free books and gifts places me under no obligation to buy anything. I can always return a shipment and cancel at any time. Even if I never buy another book, the two free books and gifts are mine to keep forever.

106 HDN ERRW   306 HDN ERRL

Name	(PLEASE PRINT)
Address	Apt. #
City	State/Prov.	Zip/Postal Code

Signature (if under 18, a parent or guardian must sign)

Mail to the **Harlequin Reader Service:**
IN U.S.A.: P.O. Box 1867, Buffalo, NY 14240-1867
IN CANADA: P.O. Box 609, Fort Erie, Ontario L2A 5X3

Not valid to current subscribers of Harlequin Presents books.

Want to try two free books from another line?
Call 1-800-873-8635 or visit www.morefreebooks.com.

* Terms and prices subject to change without notice. N.Y. residents add applicable sales tax. Canadian residents will be charged applicable provincial taxes and GST. Offer not valid in Quebec. This offer is limited to one order per household. All orders subject to approval. Credit or debit balances in a customer's account(s) may be offset by any other outstanding balance owed by or to the customer. Please allow 4 to 6 weeks for delivery. Offer available while quantities last.

Your Privacy: Harlequin Books is committed to protecting your privacy. Our Privacy Policy is available online at www.eHarlequin.com or upon request from the Reader Service. From time to time we make our lists of customers available to reputable third parties who may have a product or service of interest to you. If you would prefer we not share your name and address, please check here. ☐

HP08R

I ♥ HARLEQUIN Presents

BROUGHT TO YOU BY FANS OF
HARLEQUIN PRESENTS.

We are its editors and authors
and biggest fans—and we'd
love to hear from YOU!

Subscribe today to our online blog at
www.iheartpresents.com